About Apollo Africa

The original Heinemann African Writers Series was launched in 1962 with the publication of Chinua Achebe's *Things Fall Apart*, Cyprian Ekwensi's *Burning Grass* and Kenneth Kaunda's *Zambia Shall Be Free*, with Achebe himself acting as an editorial advisor. Over the next 40 years, the series continued to publish the best writing from across the African continent.

One of the founding aims of the Heinemann series was to make books by African writers available to as wide a readership as possible. Apollo Africa – a collaboration between Black Star Books and Head of Zeus – is proud to continue this work, ensuring novels, essays, poetry and plays from the original series are once again made available to readers all over the world.

A Few Nights and Days

A Few Nights and Days

Mbella Sonne Dipoko

Black Star Books and Head of Zeus would like to thank the following organisations: The Miles Morland Foundation, The Ford Foundation, and Africa No Filter. This publication was made possible through their support.

First published by Harlow: Longmans in 1966

Published in the Heinemann African Writers Series in 1970 by Heinemann Educational Publishers

This edition published in 2024 by Black Star Books and Head of Zeus, part of Bloomsbury Publishing Plc.

Copyright © Mbella Sonne Dipoko, 1966

The moral right of Mbella Sonne Dipoko to be identified as the author of this work has been asserted in accordance with the Copyright, Designs and Patents Act of 1988.

All rights reserved. No part of this publication may be reproduced, stored in a retrieval system, or transmitted in any form or by any means, electronic, mechanical, photocopying, recording, or otherwise, without the prior permission of both the copyright owner and the above publisher of this book.

This reprint is published by arrangement with Pearson Education Limited.

This is a work of fiction. All characters, organizations, and events portrayed in this novel are either products of the author's imagination or are used fictitiously.

9 7 5 3 1 2 4 6 8

A catalogue record for this book is available from the British Library.

ISBN (PB): 9781035900770
ISBN (E): 9781803288239

Typeset by Siliconchips Services Ltd UK

Printed and bound in Great Britain by
CPI Group (UK) Ltd, Croydon CR0 4YY

Head of Zeus Ltd
First Floor East
5–8 Hardwick Street
London EC1R 4RG

WWW.HEADOFZEUS.COM

*Onola Mbango na Ebeny'a Mbapp'a Bwanga
na Ma Ngongo na Ma Ema na M'Elong*

Chapter One

'DOUMBE, why don't you want to meet my parents?' Thérèse asked. We were in bed.

She was nineteen. She liked to carry her hair long over her shoulders and back. She was a geography student. She was slender, but broad-hipped. She didn't like her hips. She would have liked them to be narrow; and she was big at her backside—heavy there really; and that too she didn't like at all. From the start I was very fond of her. She had such an attractive face; simple eyes and rounded lips.

'Your parents?' I asked.

'Yes. Why don't you want to meet them?'

Her father had a firm in Africa, in the Ivory Coast.

'One of these days.'

'But when?'

'I don't know … Give me a bit …'

'*Non!*' she protested.

'*Allons!*'

'When will you meet them? At least my mother?'

'I've told you, one of these days.'

'But when?'

'I'll tell you after ...'
'You always say that.'
'Yes.'
'Yes what?'
I breathed deeply—in, then out.
'Listen ...'
'Why are you in such a hurry? It won't run away.'
'You too are in a hurry. Your parents won't run away.'
'But, Doumbe, I can't understand you.'
'Come on. You'll understand me after.'
'Yes! I'm no longer naïve.'
'But, Thérèse!'
'When will you meet *maman*?'
I didn't reply. After a minute or two of silence, I sighed:
'Umm.'
'Umm what?' she asked. 'You won't reply?'
'Next week, all right?'
'*Sûr?*'
'Umm.'
'*Sûr, sûr?*'
'Yes.'

Her feelings for me were a mixture of love and gratefulness; mine were tinged with a profound sense of responsibility. I was the first man to touch her and talk to her of desire. When I had said she was pretty she said I was lying. If she were pretty why didn't the boys talk to her? I told her that there was no hurry in those things. She replied that some girls got married at fifteen. Many girls began going out with boys at sixteen, even earlier. But she had been alone. Alone. She hadn't even girl friends until nine months ago when her mother took on Bibi, a Swedish girl who did house-keeping for them in exchange for board and lodging and a few francs.

Thérèse liked Bibi very much. It was through Bibi that I met Thérèse. I had gone to a dance and had asked a girl to dance with me. As we danced she said her name was Bibi; and I told her my name. I had then dropped a hint to the effect that I wanted to become acquainted. But she said she had a French boy friend so she couldn't be more than ordinary friends with me. I said that was all right with me.

Then one day I saw her on the Boulevard Saint Michel with another girl—Thérèse. I talked to Bibi and she introduced Thérèse to me. We went into a café and talked and joked and laughed. Bibi went to the telephone box. That was when I told Thérèse that she shouldn't be surprised; but I thought I liked her. I meant it. I would love to see her, alone, I said, sometime. How about her meeting me in that same café the following day? At three in the afternoon?

She said she didn't know whether or not she would be able to make it.

Bibi returned from the telephone box.

I told her that I thought her friend was charming. I really meant it.

Bibi put her hand maternally on Thérèse's shoulder, and tilted her head sideways to look into Thérèse's face.

Thérèse was shy.

The next day she turned up for the date in that same café. That was how it began.

Now it wasn't only meeting Thérèse. I had to meet her parents as well, at least her mother, as she herself had just said.

I knew what that meant. I wasn't really against it; but I didn't want to be rushed into anything, or rather rushed into it, since I knew what meeting her parents would mean; what it could lead to. I liked Thérèse very much and her profound sense of solitude made me feel very much attached to her. I thought she had even more need for me than she seemed to realize. I had taught her to hope, taught her to esteem herself a little more and she didn't hide the fact that she was grateful to me for it.

I had also taught her to dance and now she simply adored it. I also talked to her of my ancestors, the little I knew about them, and Thérèse listened. She was very broad-minded, Thérèse, very broad-minded indeed. I talked to her of the Africa of my childhood and she simply liked it. I told her the story of Mboke and Ewudu. She loved it; she said it was like a novel. She liked to hear me talk of Africa.

We also talked about Greece and Rome. But we weren't history students, so we only talked about generalities. I had a critical attitude. Sometimes I would taunt her about the militarism of Sparta; would talk about tire endless wars which were fought in the European past, wars which were the ancestors of the more recent wars of our time. But not once did she hit back and say African tribes also fought each other, that Africans fought wars against each other.

I don't know why she wasn't critical of Africa. Perhaps she had come to see Africa as something virginal, something perfect and she didn't want to tamper with that image. Or perhaps she didn't want to offend me. She was very polite with me.

I talked to her about African art and we read quite a bit on it. She even began to say perhaps she should have done ethnography or ethnology instead of geography. She said she would have loved to study a region of Africa. I once mentioned it to an African friend of mine, a science student. He was a funny chap. He said of course; didn't I know? Love was the best of ambassadors. I was really putting Africa across. I didn't like that very much because it seemed to me he said it with a touch of irony, and I am rather sensitive.

Thérèse would have told me many things; I would have learnt a lot from her if only she had a little more self-confidence. And when that self-confidence began to come, we were so involved with each other that the world didn't just seem interesting enough to talk about. We discussed ourselves, our problems. But while the old relationship lasted I talked to her of Africa and she listened with much interest. Being a geography student she would have talked to me about the regions of Europe; about the rivers, for example. But I didn't even encourage her. I didn't care for any river but the Mungo River, in Cameroon, and about that I talked. The seasons—the dry season and the rainy season. The canoe-men and their women. My childhood by that river. River of desire. River of love-songs sung by the canoe-men and their women. Welcoming river.

But nineteen years was rather too young. I was twenty-three, hard in my own way, sometimes reckless and often I thought of life as a tough adventure which called for as little sentimentality as possible. I didn't subscribe to ordinary morals and I didn't care. I lived. I had crossed oceans and deserts, burst through horizons. And all that needed audacity. Life wasn't a simple thing, nor was love: complications always developed. But to Thérèse life was hope, a refuge.

Now I was looking into her eyes and she gazed at my excitement, at first smiling, then with something like a helpless sadness. I saw love in her eyes with all the old fears and demands for reassurance. But her face showed the familiar willingness, the aroused desire and I lowered my face to hers, forgetting all that life held of distances, conscious only of nearness, warmth, desire. Her body seemed to weaken; then it became taut, throbbing with the force of her receptive tenderness. Nearness, warmth and desire with no thoughts of distances!

But later when we were once more calm and reasonable I tried to withdraw the promise I had made only a few minutes ago.

'Thérèse,' I said, 'don't you think this question of meeting your mother is rather delicate?'

'*Ça y est!*' she said. 'You have begun stalling. How is it delicate?'

'Well—'

'You're not going to tell me you're afraid.'

'Shut up. Me? Afraid? What of?'

'*Alors*, why don't you want to meet her? You said a while ago that you'd meet her next week. Now you want to change.'

'Does she know about us?'

'Yes.'

'Yes?'

'Yes. I had to tell her.'

'You didn't have to.'

'Well I have done so. She knows.' 'I thought you said she's very Catholic?'

'Yes and so?'

In the past she wouldn't have been so snappy.

'I was wondering how someone as Catholic as you say she is would take the news. Did you tell her that we do this?' I pointed at her thighs … 'She knows?'

'Of course!'

'That is something. How did you begin? I wouldn't know how to talk about it to my mother if I were a girl. Come on, tell me. How did you present it?'

'I told her I knew a boy. She wanted to know if he was nice.'

'But I am nice, my dear!'

'It's not true, wicked you.'

'Is that what you told her?'

'No. I said the boy was nice. Then she said I should be careful. She said I shouldn't go to your place. I laughed. You can't imagine how it made me laugh. She wanted to know why I was laughing. But I wouldn't tell her. She insisted. So I told her. I said her advice had come too late. *Alors là!* It was total panic, Her face red, she asked me if by that I meant you had *known* me. I said it was done.'

'What did she say?'

'She wept.'

'You shouldn't have told her.'

'But she wanted to know. I wasn't going to give her the details. It was she who asked for them.'

'And she said she wanted to see me?'

'Not immediately. She went to her room to weep. Luckily papa wasn't at home. When she later left her room she came and knocked on the door of mine. I let her in determined to tell her off should it be necessary. She sat on my bed. Then she asked me if I was expecting a child. I couldn't help laughing. I don't know why. She wanted to know why I was laughing, if by that too I meant her anxiety had come a bit late. I said no. I wasn't laughing because of that. But was I pregnant? I said no. She thanked God … It's after all normal, all that. I understand her, but I have my life. It's mine, my life. I think she has understood that now.'

'So it wasn't she who asked you to introduce me?'

'No. It's me. Does it really bother you very much? I thought it would be nice for you to meet them.'

'Does your father know?'

'My father!'

'Yes.'

'But no!'

I climbed down from the bed and went into the bathroom, splashed some water on me, wiped myself with a towel and returned to the room in a dressing gown.

It was a large room. A double bed. A table at which I worked and a chair. One large leather chair. A sideboard. A bookshelf and an enormous wardrobe with a misty mirror fitted against its door.

The dressing gown I was wearing was slightly over-size. It was a birthday present from Thérèse. I hadn't a dressing gown and she said I had to have one. Her father had dressing gowns. A man must always have a dressing gown, she said. I told her that I wasn't her father, that in Africa people used loincloths. She said it didn't matter. So when my birthday came, in February, she bought the dressing gown for me. I kissed her, sincerely, twice, on the cheek even though kissing wasn't a habit of mine. I told her it wasn't done back home. She said that was curious. She was happy that I liked the resent. A good girl with a good heart, that Thérèse. She wasn't mean, and I liked it that she wasn't.

Personally, I spent money without thinking of the next day. I expected others to be like me. Someone once said it was because there was something of an artist in me. Another person said it was because I was born in February, towards the end. I don't know much about horoscopes. But people said it was fun.

One night, at the drug store in the Champs Elysées I saw two women looking through a bundle of pamphlets on the subject. They laughed, reading through the pamphlets. They weren't middle-aged women. They were older than that; those high society women who wanted to remain young forever because of the next fashion shows. They were lightly perfumed and their faces were carefully made-up. The effect wasn't bad at all. Perhaps they had spent up to forty years learning how to put their faces in order. They held their heads together, reading one of the books which purported to talk about the present and the future in prophetic terms. I was looking through the paperbacks which lined the shelves, mostly novels. I liked to touch books. As I raised my head and looked in the direction of the women, they laughed and nudged each other. One of them selected a second horoscope pamphlet, since they already had one which had made them laugh. It was in the hands of the taller woman.

'*Ça nous amusera,*' the other woman laughed, and winked at her friend ... But life is such a tragic thing. To attain the age when one can turn only to things like horoscopes for amusement!

When I talked to Thérèse about the two women, she said she wouldn't want to live to that age. Forty would be enough for her, she said. '*Grand maximum.*' That was the way she put it. That was over a month ago. I knew she hadn't changed her mind. It was strange how morose she could be and then how elated she could suddenly become the following day. Thérèse! I knew love was a burden to her. But it was an agreeable burden. She was very delicate. Sometimes I wondered whether she realized to what extent love was an adventure. To her it seemed to be a refuge against the bitterness of the world; to me it wasn't a destination but a stop exposed to winds, to thunders, a stop exposed to storms, a stop among other stops between the first day and the last day in the life of every man and woman. I wished Thérèse could realize that we were only friends.

'Are you getting up or not?' I asked.

She passed her fingers through her hair and pouted.

'I am tired,' she said, as if moaning. 'I'll stay for a while.'

She drew the bed-clothes to her chest and tucked their edges under her armpits. Her hands weren't under the bed-clothes; so with one of them, she tapped the edge of the bed, meaning I should sit down, there!

'Come and sit down, here, here,' she said, now only caressing the edge of the bed with her fingers, tapping away, lightly, with one finger, then with another.

'I'm coming,' I said and went to the window.

I drew the curtains apart.

Daylight rushed into the room with the freshness of mid May. The sun was on the wall of the building opposite my window ... No. The sun was only on the upper storey of the building. To my right, where a little street cut at right angles with the street under my window, the red-brick wall of a tall building was fully sun-lit.

Behind the building the sky was a blotchy blue. The sky leaned over Paris. Looking at it, I felt alone, profoundly alone. I turned round and went and sat down on the edge of the bed. Thérèse took my hand in hers. Then she held my fingers to her lips and bit them, lightly.

It didn't hurt at all. It tickled, and it was faintly pleasurable. Her teeth were on my fingers, or rather on my fingernails, but I felt the effect right down in me, a tickling which was rough enough to make me laugh but which also had a vague intensity that went deeper than the depth of laughter.

Then I felt the sad—no, the melancholy feeling of love. That was why I was feeling alone. But it was only a mood. If I had waited, it would have passed as it was bound to pass, and I wouldn't have committed myself as I now did.

Thérèse suddenly let go my fingers. She tucked the bedclothes farther under her armpits as if in preparation to go to sleep. She had believed, profoundly, she had convinced herself of the oneness of the world.

'I'll meet your mother next week,' I said. 'Wednesday? Will that suit you?'

'I think so,' she said and took my hand in hers and pulled me to her. My feeling of loneliness increased. I bent over her. She pulled me closer and raising her head from the pillow, she kissed me on the lips, quickly, then her head fell back on the pillow.

We went into the details. The time: five in the afternoon. The place: a café in an area in which I had once lived before moving into my present room.

Before Thérèse left my place that afternoon she reminded me that Laurent, Bibi's boy friend, and I, had promised to take them to a dance that evening. It was a Wednesday.

I said I had forgotten. She said I forgot everything. I laughed, having recovered from my feeling of loneliness. She smiled. Then she reminded me—or thought she was reminding me—that the rendezvous was at Laurent's place, at nine that evening. She and Bibi would join us there.

I hadn't forgotten. Only I liked to pull her leg. Thérèse was nineteen and very nice. She had a pretty face, but her broad hips and large buttocks embarrassed her. They made her miserable.

Chapter Two

LAURENT lived in a little studio in a ramshackle building not far from the Place d'Italie. The ground-floor lobby and even the winding and narrow staircase smelt of garbage. The light which shone on me as I went upstairs was pale, and there was either noise or music or both behind low doors on each landing. The noise of conversation behind one of the doors was tremendous and a record which was tuned high could also be heard. It was Arab Music. Many Arabs lived in the Place d'Italie area.

I knocked on Laurent's door.

He opened it.

'*Tiens*, come in,' he said. 'I was just thinking of you. I was wondering if you'd remember about tonight.'

I went in.

'Thérèse reminded me,' I said, 'not that I had forgotten; but I had no intention of going out dancing tonight.'

'You saw her?' he asked, sitting down on a chair by a pile of records.'

The place was as usual in great disorder.

'Yes. She was at my place.'

'When?'

'This afternoon.'

'So they'll come?'

'Yes.'

'I wasn't sure. I'm no longer sure you know. Bibi's becoming unpredictable.'

'Ah?'

'It's true.'

'I think they'll come.'

He looked older than his twenty years. He led a rough life. He didn't take enough care of himself. He was an artist. He was in the Ecole Nationale des Beaux Arts. He was always dressed in a pair of trousers and a heavy pullover—when it was cold—over which he wore a leather jacket. He had three leather jackets of different colours.

Laurent was slender. He was proud and wretched at the same time. The studio in which he lived wasn't his. It was his friend's. Marc was doing his military service so Laurent took his place. He didn't pay any rent. Marc's father was an industrialist in Marseilles. But Marc was in love with Laurent, true! So he had left the studio to him. It was a year now since Marc had begun his military service and, according to Bibi, Laurent feared his return. He wondered how Marc would take the news of what had happened to him; that he, Laurent, no longer could let a man sleep with him. It was Bibi who had done that for him—at least that was what Bibi claimed for herself. And since it was she who had destroyed the affair between Laurent and Marc, she felt a great responsibility for him, for Laurent was an orphan and didn't want to work.

He was always broke, Laurent, and I don't know how he would have managed without Bibi. It was the girl who gave him money from time to time. Not much. But it helped. And now that he would no longer tolerate Marc when the rich boy returned from the army, Laurent didn't even know where he would stay. He couldn't afford one hundred and fifty francs rent for a room. He was always broke and he didn't seem to care. What was good about him was that he wasn't as closed as many French people are. It was amazing how he always wanted to behave above his age. Not only did Laurent have a long face, but he was also long-limbed.

Thérèse told me that Bibi cared very much for him. Or maybe it was the great satisfaction of having returned a man to normal intimate life that flattered her. The new Laurent had come out of her, like a child. She was very maternal towards him.

It didn't matter one bit that she had refused me six weeks ago because of that Laurent. I always told myself that I hadn't tried hard enough; and then Bibi was a foreign girl. It was normal that she should want to play up the fact that she was going out with a French boy. Foreign girls in Paris were like that. However, it didn't matter. I had Thérèse and I liked her very much. Perhaps if Bibi had let me become intimate with her it might not have been possible with Thérèse. There was nothing to regret;

and Laurent was a nice boy. It was funny, though, that he looked and behaved above his twenty years.

The studio was really dirty. Newspapers and other pieces of paper were on the floor. The ashtray was packed full of cigarette butts and ash. The plastic curtain which served as the kitchen door was drawn aside. From where I sat I could see the disorder in which the kitchen was. Newspapers as well as fruit and potato peelings were on the floor. It was difficult to imagine that Laurent couldn't clean the place in which he lived, for he looked so vigorous. It was hard to think of him as a lazy man. But he was an artist. Perhaps he didn't care or didn't want to care. Some people are like that.

'*Ça va mal au Congo!*' Laurent said. 'You saw what's in *Le Monde*?'

'Yes.'

Laurent was a communist. Perhaps he wasn't altogether a communist. But he shouted with communist students during demonstrations.

His reactions to what was happening in Africa were exactly like those of most African students in Paris. That was one of the reasons why I liked him. I could trust him. He was white but he talked and thought and hoped like an African nationalist. I was myself sufficiently to the Left to understand and appreciate his solidarity with us. He was one of the few friends I made in France. He was sincere, sensitive and hospitable.

That evening we talked a lot about the Congo and

Vietnam and he got very worked up. He finally lit himself a cigarette which he smoked in silence.

Paris. It wasn't only books. It was also dreams of a better world. That was one of the things that made us feel important in spite of our problems, and difficulties. Meeting people from different parts of the world, talking to them. One lived and hoped. One hated and loved. Moments of courage and then of despair; days of loneliness until someone's daughter brought her body and sometimes her heart as well; until a woman, ignoring the ring on her linger, agreed to offer love or her body which, quoting philosophers, she passionately asserted was hers and she could make use of just as she liked. Those agendas! The pocket note-books with addresses of hearts and bodies!

A knock on the door.

'*Tiens*,' Laurent said, rising. 'There they are.'

He strode to the door and opened it.

'Is Doumbe there?' Thérèse asked.

'First come in,' Laurent scolded. 'So you've come at last.'

Thérèse saw me. She spun on her heel to face Laurent who kissed her on the cheek, then he kissed Bibi. He put his arms on their shoulders and led them forward.

I didn't get up. Thérèse bent down and gave me her cheek. I kissed it lightly; then Bibi's cheek. I also kissed it.

'He won't even get up,' Bibi said.

'You don't know him,' Thérèse said. 'He's the most ill-bred boy on earth.'

'It's not late to begin his re-education,' Laurent said,

dropping into the chair he had been occupying when the girls knocked on the door. 'But it would need a really good teacher which I don't think any of you is. You two have so much need to be taught.'

'*Mais*,' growled Thérèse, flinging her handbag on the bed.

She sat down on the bed.

'*Si*,' said Laurent. 'You still have to learn to be on time.'

Thérèse shrugged. 'It's not our fault—'

'Laurent,' Bibi remonstrated, looking at the room with disgust. 'Look at where you live. You won't change.'

'Another re-education,' I laughed.

'They must be reformed, both of them,' said Thérèse who leaned to me to lay her fingers on my cheek, pushing it playfully. 'Especially this one. The worst character you can ever think of.'

'Laurent is worse,' Bibi said, shaking her head. 'He lives in a dust bin.'

'Say *we* live in a dust bin,' Laurent said, smiling. 'And besides, really well-brought up women wouldn't waste their time talking. They'd put the house in order. How many times have I told you that? I don't care. But if you care, then you should clean the place. I've always told you so. But you won't learn.'

'It looks as though it's not only one person who's got to be re-educated and reformed, but all of us,' Thérèse remarked, crossing her legs. 'Eh, Doumbe, what do you think about that?'

I thought she was insinuating at what Bibi was supposed to have done to Laurent, what she claimed she had done to him.

'I don't know,' I said, and, to change the subject, I asked, 'Why did you come late?'

'*Ça y est!*' Thérèse exclaimed, getting up. 'They're howling from all corners, the men. The Métro broke down—'

We were all changing. We didn't have to be changed, to be re-educated, to be reformed. That had been done, already. Thérèse for example, who had been innocent and shy had begun to talk, even to mock at men. It was true that she did it playfully; but the point was that she did it. In the past she had been glum and docile; now she too was talking. But it would be incorrect to say she had changed of her own. My influence was there. She too was influencing me; for I was beginning to become sentimental about women—about her—something I had decided I couldn't do.

Bibi began to clean the room. She picked up the newspapers which were scattered on the floor and took them to the kitchen. She returned with a broom and swept the room.

'What do you think you're doing there?' Laurent asked, as if he hadn't eyes. 'Is it here we're going to dance?'

After Bibi finished putting the studio in order, we went out. We took the Métro. It was Laurent who suggested the dance hall we went to. Bibi and Thérèse were out on the pretext that they were going to see a film. It was because of Thérèse. A lie was necessary for her parents to allow her to go out with Bibi at night.

'If your mother asks you what the film was about, what would you say, Thérèse?' I asked as we were surfacing at the Bastille.

Bibi laughed.

'After all the films one has seen,' she said, 'there'd always be something to say.'

'She won't even ask,' Thérèse said. 'She has confidence in me.'

'Of course!' I said. 'Why not?'

'But it's true.'

'I didn't say it wasn't. All the same, assuming she asked?'

'I'd talk to her about a film I saw two days ago, in the afternoon.'

'I don't want you to be lying, Thérèse.'

'*Ça y est!*' she cried. 'The orders have begun, *la morale* ... I have my life, no? I can do whatever I like. I can lie if it so pleases me. How does it affect you? And besides, you yourself, you lie like anything.'

She couldn't have said that in the past. Then she had listened, had talked very little and rarely contradicted me.

Bibi had taken Laurent's arm. They walked in front of us. Laurent had a boastful way of walking. He bore himself straight, almost stiffly.

'Thérèse I don't like it when you talk like that,' I said, morosely.

'It was you who began it,' she grumbled.

'I detest this idea of your having your own life. It doesn't fit in with what I think of you.'

Bibi and Laurent turned to the left.

Thérèse took my arm. She easily regretted the things she said to me as soon as she saw that they had offended me. Although she was weaker than I, she behaved as though my temper were an egg which had to be handled with care, with the result that it seemed as though it was I who was the weaker of the two of us. She was such a sweet young girl.

We also branched off to the left. Bibi and Laurent crossed the street and walked on the opposite pavement. Thérèse and I did the same.

Bibi was a big woman, big. She was Laurent's height. They were taller than Thérèse and I. Thérèse was my height; no, she was slightly taller. It's not true. It's the high-heel shoes she wore that made her look as though she were taller than I by an inch or so. Thérèse liked Bibi very much. Bibi was a good-natured young woman. She was twenty-three.

Bibi and Laurent turned to the right. Bibi was big without being large.

Thérèse and I also turned to the right, into a narrow street.

Prostitutes in tight-fitting dresses leaned against the

counter in the cafés and bars which were on both sides of the rather dimly-lit street.

Bibi and Laurent got to the entrance of the dance hall. They went in.

Thérèse and I also went in.

We bought our tickets and a waiter in a white jacket showed us a free table. We sat down and he asked us what we would drink. Beer for Laurent and Bibi; fruit juice for Thérèse and me. Bibi paid for her beer and Laurent's. I paid for the fruit juice. We talked and laughed and looked at the dancers.

The band played from a flood-lit balcony. A cha-cha-cha. The walls of the dance hall were beautifully decorated. You thought you were looking at log cabins.

I asked Thérèse for a dance. We got up and went onto the floor.

We had been dancing for a few minutes when I noticed that Laurent and Bibi were dancing quite near us. Bibi must have been watching us. She smiled at me when our eyes met. I smiled back, then I smiled at Thérèse who seemed already to be enjoying herself.

After the cha-cha-cha we returned to our seats.

Then the complications began. I surprised Laurent making eyes at Thérèse. I pretended I hadn't seen anything. The lights dimmed. From the ceiling a large disc covered with blue bulbs began to revolve as the band struck up a tango.

'Thérèse, let's dance,' Laurent said, getting up.

Thérèse hesitated. She consulted me with her eyes. I raised my hands in the direction of the dance floor, meaning she should go ahead and dance.

Laurent grabbed her arm and pulled her with mock impatience. She got up and followed him.

They began to dance.

A tango isn't a very happy dance. It is full of sophisticated melancholy.

Laurent and Thérèse were soon lost in the crowd.

'Won't you dance?' Bibi asked me.

'Why, are you jealous?' I laughed.

'No. I don't think so.'

'That's good.'

'Why?'

'Oh, Bibi, one bothers oneself for nothing you know.'

'By being jealous?'

'Yes.'

'You sound it, you.'

'Do I?'

She nodded.

She lit a cigarette and dropped the match stick in an ashtray she had taken from the table next to ours. She leaned forward, her left elbow on the table, left cheek against her left palm. She was literally blowing the smoke into my face.

'What do you think you're doing?' I asked, liking the expression in her eyes. It was a mature expression, bold. But a certain oblique reserve lurked in it.

'What am I doing?' she asked; then, smoking, she closed her eyes.

'Yes. What do you think you're doing?'

She took the cigarette between her fingers, threw her head backwards and blew the smoke into the air. She put out her tongue, not completely, but enough for me to have seen it between her lips. The effect was provocative. She smiled a drunken woman's smile. But she wasn't drunk. The reserve that had been in her eyes disappeared.

'Smoking,' she said. 'You want to try one?'

'No thanks,' I said.

'You don't smoke; you don't drink. What then do you do?'

'Nothing. And besides, never say that to a man who doesn't smoke and drink. Never ask him what then does he do.'

She understood and smiled; glanced at me, then smoked for a minute without saying anything.

The tango.

Bibi put her cigarette in the ashtray and pinned her right elbow, like the left, on the table; wrists against each other, she carried her chin and cheeks in her palms, her fingers spread on her cheeks. She stared into my eyes.

'Tell me,' she said, the corner of her upper lip twitching, 'do you love Thérèse?'

'Why do you ask?'

'Why not?'

'Do you love Laurent?'

'Very much!'
'And you're not even smiling.'
'Why should I smile?'
'Because you're lying.'
'What makes you think I am lying?'
'Because you're lying …'

She sat up, took her cigarette and smoked in silence. Then, taking it between her fingers she blew the smoke into the air and said: 'You mean I don't love Laurent?'

'That is what I mean.'
'But do you love Thérèse?'
'Since you want to know—'
'Yes. I do want to know. Do you love her?'
'I don't know.'
'What don't you know?'
'If I love her or not.'
'Men!'
'What have they done again?'
'Why do you sleep with her if you don't love her?'
'I like her very much, as a person. I am very fond of her.'
'You think that is enough?'
'For now, yes. You, why do you let Laurent sleep with you if you don't love him?'
'Because it may come.'
'What proves that the same is not true of me?'
'But Thérèse loves you.'
'The more reason why I should sleep with her.'
'Why?'

'Because, as you say, she loves me. You just said why should

I do it with her when I don't love her.'

'Certainly—'

'Wait. To you it should be done only when there is love.'

'Exactly.'

'You don't sound convinced. You're not kidding?'

'Me? Kidding? Why?'

'Well you sound it. But it doesn't matter, I was saying that, since according to you it should be done only when there is love, Thérèse has every right to do it, because she is in love.'

'But you aren't.'

'I agree. Would she have to wait until I too fell in love with her?'

'Yes.'

'Listen, Bibi, you're not serious.'

'Of course I am. You know I'm serious.'

'I don't know.'

I imagine she was enjoying herself, talking like that. We had never been so free with each other before. In the past she had a certain reserve which I didn't altogether like. Sometimes I thought she didn't like me. Now we were talking like good friends.

I looked away from her and gazed at the dancing on the floor. It was awkward. The tango is a very difficult dance. Most of the couples stood on the spot and swayed; others walked as rhythmically as they could manage.

A few danced well, taking real tango steps and it was beautiful to watch. But those who couldn't dance it as it should be danced improvised or danced as if it were a blues or even a fox-trot.

Many took very long steps, outpacing the tango. But they all seemed to be enjoying themselves, and that was the essential thing. Did it matter whether or not one danced the tango like a fox-trot? The thing was to let a man be there, on the floor, a woman in his arms; let a woman be there, a man before her; and let the band put that music out of the accordion, the violin, the bass … with that voice singing of the heart.

I turned my eyes back to Bibi and asked:

'Bibi, what do you think of yourself?'

I honestly don't know why I suddenly asked that question.

'What do I think of myself?' she mused.

'Yes,' I said, nodding, feeling a bit bored.

Her eyes narrowed. She frowned.

'What do you think of yourself, you?' she asked, rather contemptuously.

I thought for a while, then I said, 'I think of myself as only a tender-hearted person in a hard world—'

'False modesty,' she spat.

'What's modest about that?'

'You must say what you believe in. You must say what you think of yourself, just exactly as you feel. Now, don't tell me you believe what you said just now.'

'I can say something. You can't. I asked you the same question. You didn't reply.'

'I think I am an ugly woman in an ugly world.'

'Do you believe what you've just said?'

'Of course I believe it.'

'But you know you're not ugly. Why do you lie?'

'I'm not lying.'

It wasn't only one tango. It was a series of tangos.

A bulky woman with a white handbag dangling from her arm danced with a slender man quite near to our table. The woman was short. She was extravagantly made-up. She was neckless. Her head rested on her shoulder and she had a very large bosom. But she looked very happy. She wore a permanent smile. The man didn't look so happy. He wasn't smiling. Bibi also watched them.

'Listen, Bibi,' I said.

'Yes?'

'I want to tell you something.'

'Go ahead.'

'I know it's wrong; but I don't mind.'

'What?'

'I think I'm still interested in you.'

'What do you mean?'

'Don't pretend. You know what I mean.'

She looked at the cigarette between her fingers.

'You want to make love to me, is that it?' she asked.

'Not so bluntly, Bibi.'

She smiled and closed her eyes and smoked her cigarette
When her mouth was free, she said:

'I thought it was over since you met Thérèse. I thought you were no longer interested.'

She sounded flattered.

'I still am,' I said.

'But I'm sorry, Doumbe. I'm not in the least interested in you.'

'Because of Laurent?'

'Why because of Laurent?'

'Because last time it was because of him.'

'No. I like you very much; but that is all. And then Thérèse loves you. You must try to be faithful to her.'

'Good advice; damn good advice. After all …'

'It's true.'

'I know.'

'No. You sound sarcastic.'

'Why? Anyway, let's change the subject. Will you be free tomorrow afternoon?'

'Why do you ask?'

'Listen, there's something I want to discuss with someone, any person really; but certainly not with Thérèse. I don't know if you understand.'

'No. I don't.'

'I'd like to tell you something, a kind of secret. Thérèse mustn't know.'

'Tell me now.'

She was smiling.

'Don't think it's in connection with what we've been talking about.'

'Oh, no! Never!' she cried. 'How could it ever be?'

'You're kidding.'

'Am I?'

'Bibi,' I said gravely. 'I like people to be serious when I'm serious. It's so exasperating when people joke about things that shouldn't be treated lightly. I hate it. When I say I want to discuss something with you that has nothing to do with love or things like that, I mean it. I do. You understand?'

'Well, okay, what's it about?'

'I asked you if you'd be free tomorrow afternoon.'

'Yes.'

'I'd wait for you at home, around five. Don't tell Thérèse. Don't imagine anything. I'm not what you probably think I am. I'd be myself with you. I very much want to take you into my confidence.'

I knew she knew what I meant. But I also knew that she imagined I thought she didn't know. It was better to leave it at that. Those things sit very awkwardly on a woman's conscience, on some men's too, for that matter. But it's rough for a woman. They all want to appear so virtuous. So one has to make it easier for them. Even when they come willingly, in full awareness of what awaits them, make them imagine you think they are being led blindly, even when it is they who are leading you blindly into it.

'I don't think I can make it,' Bibi said.

'Nonsense!' I snarled. 'You said you'd be free tomorrow. Because I said I wanted to take you into my confidence? You're scared?'

'I'm not scared.'

I laughed. 'Be nice, Bibi,' I said. I took her left hand in my right and gave it a gentle squeeze, let it go, then looked into her eyes. She looked back at me and it was exciting that she didn't lower her eyes.

Just then Thérèse dashed out of the crowd of dancers. She was furious and, not looking at Bibi, she bent and picked up her handbag which was under the table. Then, seizing my hand, she cried: 'Let's go. Let's go!'

I didn't get up immediately.

'What's the matter, Thérèse?' I asked. 'Eh?'

She was trembling. 'Are you coming or not?' she cried.

'Thérèse!'

'Are you coming or not?' she repeated, impatiently, stamping her foot on the floor.

'Where's Laurent?' I asked.

She let go my hand and hurried towards the exit.

'Bibi, something has gone wrong,' I said, getting up. 'See you tomorrow, at five.'

I hurried after Thérèse and caught up with her just as she was gaining the pavement.

'Thérèse!'

She didn't look back.

I put my arm round her. 'What's the matter?'

'Laurent,' she said.

'What happened?'

She didn't reply.

We walked in silence until we got to the Place de la Bastille. We entered a café and went to the back where there were usually fewer people.

We sat down.

A corpulent man sat by himself, a glass of beer before him. He was reading an evening newspaper. Then there was a woman, a pale-faced woman, who stared into space. She appeared to be counting, mentally counting, either her money or her years. To say she appeared to be counting is only a way of trying to portray her blank-faced concentration. She may only have been thinking about tomorrow, or maybe about yesterday—what had been; wondering if its return could be hoped for, knowing how lonely the days had become. Or perhaps she was only trying to do all her thinking now, while she was in the café, so that once she was in bed an hour or so later, she wouldn't have anything more to think about. It looked as though she had trouble with her sleep. She was pale and thin. She wasn't young. She had a ring on her finger. An empty glass of beer was on her table. But if she had trouble with her sleep, there were sleeping pills. Maybe she didn't like them. She wanted to do all her thinking in the café so as to free her mind, so that she would be able to sleep an hour or so later.

Thérèse also used to have trouble with her sleep; but she didn't like to take pills. One became addicted and it was bad.

I said I agreed with her. I hated those pills myself.

Like Thérèse, I also had trouble with my sleep, from time to time.

The pale-faced woman now sighed and looked at her left hand which was spread on the table.

People shouted from the counter. Others played the Flipper. The machine rattled and the spectators were noisy. From where Thérèse and I sat we couldn't see the counter; nor the Flipper.

Laughter and noise, even shouting.

'Thérèse, now tell me. What happened?'

'Oh,' she breathed, as if disgusted. 'He's a filthy fellow, Laurent. He was rubbing himself against me, and then he wanted to kiss me.'

'To kiss you?'

'Yes. And by force. He's ill. There's something the matter with him.'

'He wanted to kiss you?'

'But, yes!' Thérèse said, with force. 'He wanted me to go to his place.'

That was bad, very bad. A terrible coincidence—such as I would find difficult to believe should I happen to come across it in a novel.

'He said he wanted you to come to his place?'

'*Mais oui!* He's not well.'

'Well, I thought he was a friend.'

'A friend!'

'That's what I thought. And you say he asked you to come to his place?'

'Yes. He said he loved me.'

'No! He also said that? Tell me, Thérèse, don't you think he was joking?'

'Joking! Do you joke when you ask a girl to come to your place and you ask her not to tell anyone?'

I thought of my advances to Bibi.

'I don't understand,' I said, very embarrassed. 'What are you saying?'

'Just that—''He asked you to come to his place. When?'

'On Friday.'

'What time?'

'Lunch-time.'

'I see. So he really wanted you to come alone?'

'*Mais bien sûr.* He knows Bibi will be at home; and when she leaves the house it will be to go to her language course.'

'I think you should go and not tell Bibi anything.'

'Why?'

'I'd come and join you at Laurent's. It would be amusing to have him explain why you are there.'

'It wouldn't amuse me. I won't go.'

'Anyway, don't tell Bibi.'

'Why shouldn't I?'

'Listen, Thérèse, you know she is in love with him.'

'She's not in love with him.'

'Okay, let's say he is in love with her—'

'He's not in love with her. It's because she gives him money. And he can't be in love with her since he says he has been in love with me since he saw me.'

'He said he is in love with you?'

'Yes! It was as if to impress the fact on me that he wanted to kiss me.'

'He said that …'

Thérèse took one of my hands in hers as if to reassure me, when she might well have been weeping instead had she known what I had been saying to Bibi.

Thérèse wase lovingly naïve. Not that she could have known that I had asked Bibi to come to my place. There was no means of knowing. Our designs were safe, or rather my designs, for there was still no means of knowing whether or not Bibi would turn up. But even if Thérèse had known, and I had told her that I wouldn't do such a thing again, she would only have asked if I was sure I wouldn't start again. I would have promised and Thérèse would have believed me. She was younger in mind than her nineteen years. I didn't like that at all. It aroused pity in me, like now, as she held my hand in hers, trying to reassure me.

I faintly regretted having flirted with Bibi, and was uneasy at the thought of what might follow, should she come to my place the following day.

Thérèse was so good to me and yet I couldn't be faithful

to her. Already there was Ndome, an African girl; and soon, who knew, there would be Bibi.

'Don't be sad,' Thérèse said. 'I shall love no one else.'

Oh, no, Thérèse …

Chapter Three

'I'm sorry I'm late,' Bibi said, putting her handbag on the table.

Her skirt had profuse pleats. They hid her curves. She sat down on the bed.

'I am very glad you came,' I said.

'Since you said it was important. But tell me. What was wrong with Thérèse last night?'

'Nothing serious,' I said. 'You know how impulsive she is at times.'

'Did Laurent misbehave himself?'

'No. Why? What put the idea into your head?'

'Well I don't know. The way she came running to us.'

'Hysterics.'

'That's what you'd say.'

'But you know Thérèse—'

'I am almost certain Laurent tried something on.'

'Tried!'

'Yes.'

'It's so easy to misbehave. One doesn't have to try. One tries not to misbehave. Is that what you meant?'

'How could I have meant that?'

'Well I don't know. However it doesn't matter. That's over now. Did you stay long after we had left?'

'An hour. Perhaps less.'

'What did Laurent say?'

'About Thérèse?'

'Yes.'

'Nothing. He came towards me, laughing. When I asked him what had happened, he only said Thérèse was a child …'

'It's funny how Laurent imagines himself to be old, at twenty.'

I went and put on a record on the electrophone. Then I sat facing Bibi. She was observing me with an amused smile. Her blouse was wet at the armpits. She had such large eyes.

'Let's dance,' I said.

'No. I want to talk,' she said. 'Why are you trying to cover up Laurent?'

'Trying to cover up Laurent!'

'Yes. You know he made advances to Thérèse; that was why she was furious.'

'Who told you?'

'Thérèse.'

'And how are you sure I know about it?'

'She told me that you know. That she told you. You see,' she smiled, 'we don't hide anything from each other.'

'I see.'

'You see.'

'Umm.'

'Then why were you pretending?'

'You want to know why?'

'Yes.'

'Because I was just as guilty as he was, if one can talk of guilt in these things. If he made advances to her, what was wrong in that? I was doing the same to you. And I don't think it would be honest to get all worked up about a little incident like that, knowing what I myself was up to.'

'You know?'

'No.'

'I've been faithful to Laurent since I met him. You knew that?'

'I assumed it.'

'And the brat had the impudence—'

'Now wait a minute. Don't get worked up. You said last night that you're not jealous.'

'I know I am not; but there's a limit to everything.'

'You want to leave him?'

'Leave him?'

'Yes.'

'I could do it.'

'Don't do it. Oh, please don't.'

'Now you're joking again.'

'Honestly, don't leave Laurent. I feel it is my duty to persuade you not to leave him. Can you imagine how bad I would feel should someone ask Thérèse to leave me?'

'You think if I wanted to leave him it's what you've said that would make me change my mind?'

'No. It won't make you change your mind. Things are not as easy as that. Thérèse used to say she has her own life; I guess I have mine too, and so have you, your own life. It's not what I tell you that matters. It's what you tell yourself. But, all jokes aside, I think you shouldn't leave him. You can take a look outside, from time to time; does no harm to anyone provided the contacts are clean; but don't let him down.'

'Why?'

'I don't have to tell you, Bibi. You know Laurent has need of you, more than I do. I only desire you. But he may even love you, no matter what you and Thérèse may think.'

'What is that word you slipped in, so tactfully in that mouthful?'

'What?'

I laughed.

'You heard me.'

'You mean the word I slipped in in what I was saying just now?'

'Yes.'

'Desire?'

'Yes. Is that why you asked me to come.'

'Okay! Okay, Bibi. Yes. Let the sky fall.'

'What about the secret, the confidence?'

'But that's it. In the circumstances—I mean with Lament and Thérèse as our friends—don't you see I shouldn't be saying this to you? And that if I do, as now, it can only be a secret? Should be a secret, to spare everybody torment? And we'll need a lot of confidence between us for anything to be possible. Listen, we'd have to be careful about it. When I was a child I saw terrible things happen simply because people went with their friends' women. But human nature is stronger than memory, as if memory weren't part of that nature. I shouldn't be trying to have you, you know.'

I was hinting at the loves and the tears, the betrayals, the desire on the Mungo.

'I honestly don't think I can do that, Doumbe. Believe me.'

'But since you're going to leave Laurent—'

'I didn't say I was going to leave him. I said I could do it.'

'Oh!'

'Yes.'

'You're sure you don't want to dance?'

'Yes. I'm sure.'

'What then do you want to do?'

'Nothing.'

'You don't want to stay. You don't want to go away. You don't want to dance. You don't want not to dance. You don't want to lie down. You don't want to remain seated. Then you just don't exist. Come on, Bibi, you've got to live. You've got to do something.'

'You tell me what I should do?'

'Lie down.'

She lay down.

'What next?' she asked.

'Take off your shoes.'

She took off her shoes.

'What next?'

'I honestly don't know what next you should do. Or I know, but I don't know how to put it.'

'I think I know.'

'How to *put* it?'

'No. What next I should do.'

'And that is?'

'Sit up, and then put on my shoes.'

'You loop progress. You make things cyclic. Things, people and situations must keep on moving; we have to do things and not undo them after having done them.'

She sat up. Abstractions weren't her strong point. Philosophy didn't matter anyway. She put on her shoes.

She looked over to the window and then closed her eyes and yawned.

'Now you're bored,' I said. 'And so soon.'

'Yes. I'm bored.'

I got up and went and sat by her side, on the bed. I touched her.

'No,' she said.

'I know you don't want it.'

'Honestly I don't.'

'I do.'

I kissed her neck.

'No, Doumbe. Honestly no.'

I had heard that once. No! and I had assumed it was a true no; and I had given up. I heard later that the girl was laughing at me behind my back; she said I was a child. I have since learnt to ignore a simple no.

'Yes, Bibi,' I said in reply to her no. 'Honestly yes!'

She looked at me quickly, and smiled. I put my hand under her dress and touched her thighs. Philosophy had suddenly made her begin to yawn. And the opposite of pure thought is pure action and that was what I was up to, and I was sure it wouldn't make her yawn.

She sighed.

'No,' she said. 'I know he's unfaithful to me with other girls, but I can't. You understand?'

'Of course you can, Bibi. You know you can.'

I rose from her side and returned to the chair.

'Are you angry?' she asked.

'Why should I be angry? If you won't then why should I care? After all …'

'Listen. You're angry. Come and sit here.'

'No.'

The point is that once a woman has implied her yes, a man's no, an overt and brutal no, becomes very caustic. That is how the world is.

'Please.'

'I say no.'

She got up and came to the chair.

'You must know it isn't easy for a woman,' she said. 'It's never easy.'

'Women have always said so. Why can't we find a new language for these things?'

'Doumbe, believe me. It's not easy for a woman.'

'Because you don't want it to be easy.'

She was silent for a while. Then she asked, bluntly, even though her aspect and voice remained meek:

'Are you sure you need me?'

'No, no, no! I don't any longer. I'm sorry. It's not worth the trouble.'

'Why?'

'Because it seems I was dreaming. I'm not interested in you, true. I'm sorry. I don't think I ever was, really. I'm sorry.'

She looked at me, then turning her face away, she burst into tears.

I was touched and regretted the tactics I had used. But a woman wants a man to be able to take whatever he wants; and sometimes one tries hard, and the woman thinks one hasn't tried hard enough.

And when one tries very very hard, it makes her cry.

That could embarrass a man very much, could put before him the choice: hardness or sentimentality. Choose the former and they say you're not tender; choose the latter, and the complaint comes: you're weak. A woman can be sentimental; but she will hate a man who fawns and weeps because he loves her. The thing is, that a man mustn't be tender and humble before life. The world is a hard world. The world isn't tender. And that is what women seem to have understood; and knowing themselves, they ask for their men not to be like they are, for before the world a couple must be complementary. The woman brings tenderness, the man courage, boldness, firm resolutions, the hardness that protects, that builds, that conserves. But for a man the choice is in-between, a little sentimentality and a certain amount of hardness.

That is what I think life had given me. I was touched by Bibi's tears. I regretted the tactics I had used. The world was so hard. It was unfair to add to the suffering of people who were already suffering; and we all suffer in one way or another. That is why we have to be hard, to be able to stand it.

'Bibi,' I said, sympathetically. 'You shouldn't have cried. It disarms me. I can't do anything with you while you're in this state. You're so weak now, see! It would be unfair to take you now. I've done it once. I don't intend to do it again. It's so unfair. Wipe your tears. Stop crying. I desire you, very much. But I can't take you while you're in this state, while all your resistance has given way. It would be unfair, Bibi, unless you permit me … Do you?'

She nodded and reached out for her handbag, fetched herself a handkerchief and wiped her eyes and blew her nose. Then she replaced the handkerchief in the handbag, closed it and put it on the table. I waited for her to calm down after which I led her to the bed where she could be more comfortable. We sat down on its edge, my arm around her.

She looked up.

'The window,' she said.

I got up and went and drew the curtains.

'Doumbe, it is wrong,' she said when I returned to the bed. 'I wonder whether you understand.'

'I think I do.'

'Normally I shouldn't be doing this, but—'

'Bibi, you know I shouldn't either, because of Thérèse …'

It was from Bibi that I first heard about 'safe days'. She said that day was one of her safe days. We didn't need to take precautions. Protection was unnecessary.

'Thérèse calls it my waist-coat,' I said.

Bibi gave a little laugh. Memories. The long days spent out of Paris. The departures for Riviera holidays! Those days of books and love. The dawn in Normandy. A sun-lit dawn! Then the return to Paris. The cafés. The painters in Montmartre! I recall the loose, beautiful shame, a resigned shame which was on Bibi's face that afternoon and I think of many things. The past and the future; and the bronze light which filtered in through the curtains seems to me today, in retrospect, like the shadow of love; the melancholy shadow of the past.

'What's the matter?' Bibi asked, her hand on my chest.

'I am thinking, Bibi,' I sighed.

'About Thérèse?'

'No.'

'I know it's about her. Do you regret it?'

'Why should I regret?'

'Well I don't know. But you looked so thoughtful.'

She was right. I was thinking of Thérèse. Even though I wasn't regretting anything. I felt her solitude in the distance. Her goodness and near-innocence. What Bibi and I had just done only confirmed to me that Thérèse was an unfortunate girl. She loved me, trusted me; she loved and trusted Bibi. And there we were, both of us, betraying all the naïve confidence she had in us.

Chapter Four

THE day of the rendezvous with Thérèse and her mother came.

The café had a sombre aspect which I liked. I stopped there from time to time to have a cup of coffee, some tea or a glass of cold milk or a glass of mineral water.

Certain afternoons, I spent up to two hours there, reading. It was a relatively quiet café. There was something mutely intimate about it. The plane trees on the pavement outside cast a sombre shadow on its terrace. I would be sitting there and a tango or a waltz would rise from the juke box. It was so different from the cafés in Saint Germain des Prés. There, rowdy students ruled; here the majority of the customers were of middle-age. They shuffled in, sat down, or simply stood by the counter and had a cup of coffee or a glass of beer or some red wine. Many took it white and *sec*.

They talked about the prices and used words like inflation and expansion very freely. They also talked about the accommodation problem and they used words like investment and loans very freely. They talked about investment in real estate and many quoted statistics. Many! Perhaps it was the same fellow all the time. People patronized certain cafés and also patronized certain subjects. They went to the same café and discussed their favourite subjects. But the manager of the café participated in all the discussions. He had to; it was part of his business.

Sometimes however, as I sat in the café, a group of teenagers would arrive, talkative—boys and girls—and they talked about music-hall artists. The boys also talked about football matches, bicycle racing, swimming, skiing and even about boxing. Some demonstrated with their fists. They laughed; but they came there very rarely, those noisy boys and girls. At least I didn't see them there each time I stopped at the café. But whenever they were there, the place was noisy because they played the Flipper and shouted and laughed. They took turns at the Flipper. But they didn't take turns at the shouting. That they did collectively. And they put coins in the juke box. They didn't select tangos and waltzes and airs like that. As youngsters they went for the strident guitars and shrill voices of young stars. The boys and girls chewed away—chewing gum I guess—and it seemed as though they all wanted to look tough. Sometimes I used to wonder what they'd tell their children when the time came. After the Flippers and juke boxes and the chewing gum and the pop tunes and the flirtations how would they dare tell their kids to take it easy? Perhaps they would all the same. It didn't begin yesterday.

One day, as I was sitting in that café in which I was

now waiting for Thérèse and her mother, all the boys and girls who happened to be there that afternoon shouted at once—I don't know at what—and when their voices fell, an old man—sixty or sixty-five years old—who was drinking red wine at the counter shouted, alone, as hard as he could. Then he said:

'Ha! ha! One must do as the young do.'

That was funny. I smiled to myself. That was new; and maybe he was right. Fathers, to follow the example of their children, should shout and snap their fingers at juke boxes, play the Flipper, chew away at chewing gum, howl! But our old man was not only a father, but a grandfather trying to follow the example of youth, his grand-children; that was something. I smiled to myself.

Today, I began to wonder why Thérèse and her mother were delaying. Perhaps her mother had changed her mind; all the better.

'Monsieur?' the waiter asked.

'I'm waiting for friends,' I said.

'As you wish,' the waiter said and returned to the counter.

I thought of Bibi; then of Laurent.

Thérèse and her mother arrived and Bibi was with them. Thérèse's mother must have brought her to serve as a cover. Should an acquaintance of her husband's see us she would say that Bibi was my fiancé, if she was asked by her husband to explain her presence with her daughter in a café that afternoon in the company of an African.

Bibi had told me that Thérèse's mother was extremely nice. She didn't treat her as a maid, but rather as a daughter. I would have said almost as a daughter. Only, Bibi had said, Thérèse's mother hadn't the least confidence in herself. Perhaps it was because of her piety. The Church breaks some people. Or maybe it was because of her husband. Bibi thought both were responsible.

Monsieur Vaele, Thérèse's father, Bibi had told me, was very sensitive. I said we all were, so what? She said he was too much so. He always suspected his wife and daughter were making fun of him. And since he wouldn't have it, he insisted on his wife behaving in a way that would convince him that she respected him. This had led to a kind of tyranny. Thérèse's mother was its main victim. As for Thérèse, being an only child, Bibi had said, the result of her father's attitude was that she had developed the tactics of a spoilt child. She could be peevish, adamant, impudent. And it was her father who had come to fear her. That was what Bibi said. Thérèse had her way in nearly everything. Her father could fight back only with formal anger, a noisy explosion of invective and threats which soon gave way to endearments, for Thérèse almost invariably boycotted her parents after any serious quarrel. But it was with her father that she was always at war, and yet in her reaction she included her mother in the boycott because Madame Vaele was forced to take her husband's side. Otherwise Thérèse's father would accuse her of being against him. That was what Bibi said.

Now, there she was, Thérèse's mother, not knowing that I already knew quite a bit about her and her husband, how they were at home. She was a tall, slim woman. Through her age it was easy to see how pretty she had been some years ago.

I rose and smiled. Madame Vaele seemed to hurry forward, smiling in her turn. But there was something artificial in her smile. It was because of me that she had wept that day, when Thérèse had mentioned me. And here she was, smiling. It was certain that she hadn't brought up her daughter to end up in a foreigner's arms. All that she had done for her, all the attention, all the expenses, all the hopes were in the hope that some French boy would turn up and be her son-in-law. A Jean-Louis, a Francis, a Jean-Marie or even a Laurent. It was natural—the way the world was—that such should be her dream, which I imagined explained the artificiality of her smile.

I felt like a perturber. I hate to hurt people and there we were. From her nervous smile I knew I was already hurting her; but there was another person: her husband, who according to Thérèse, still didn't know I existed. I would have done anything to spare them suffering, and yet what could I have done? What could I have done?

Now that I am writing about it all, the phrases come quickly to mind. I would have done anything to spare them suffering—as if it was as easy as that!

No.

I couldn't have done much. To leave Thérèse would have

naturally saved her parents some of the embarrassment and suffering which was to follow; but what about the girl? I had to choose. I chose Thérèse against her parents. They could suffer. But I didn't want Thérèse to suffer.

'Doumbe, my mother,' Thérèse said rather indifferently. She wore a frown.

'I am very pleased to know you,' her mother said, shaking my hand.

'Me too,' I said.

Then I shook Thérèse's hand, then Bibi's.

Because Madame Vaele was there I didn't want to kiss Bibi and Thérèse on the cheek. I didn't kiss them. The handshake was enough. I didn't want to display too much familiarity with Thérèse in the presence of her mother. Thérèse, and then Bibi, had told me she was very Catholic. Thérèse used the adverb *fanatiquement*. So I thought the lady was already doing a lot by consenting to be introduced to me, and at that behind her husband's back. I was grateful to her for it and it didn't matter that her smile was artificial.

We sat down. Thérèse sat opposite Bibi, and I facing Thérèse's mother.

'*Alors?*' Madame Vaele said, her hands on the table. She was a bit nervous. She was making an effort to be calm.

I sensed her torment, her pain, her fear, her great uneasiness.

I smiled and signalled for the waiter to come. He hurried to our table, an empty tray in his left hand.

'What will you have, madame?' I asked Thérèse's mother.

She glanced at Bibi.

'I don't even know,' she said. She shrugged her shoulders and added: '*Bon*, fruit juice.'

'Orange? Grape? Pine-apple?' the waiter recited.

'Pine-apple.'

'Bibi?'

'A coffee.'

'Thérèse?'

'Coffee.'

I looked up at the waiter and said:

'Three coffees and some fruit juice—pine-apple.'

The waiter went to the counter.

'Thérèse, what's the matter?' I asked. 'You don't look pleased. Madame you haven't been cross with her I suppose?'

'Not at all,' Madame Vaele said, looking at her daughter. 'Perhaps she's a bit tired.'

'I don't want to be sentimental but I am forced to be, just a little bit. I am highly touched that you accepted to meet me.'

'Nothing could be more natural,' Thérèse's mother said.

I knew that wasn't entirely true. But politeness was a mass attitude. It didn't take the individual into consideration, or his susceptibility. Politeness saved the individual from being unnecessarily hurt. But its language was like ready-made clothes. Even worse. They saved trouble and time. But they fitted badly sometimes. It was natural that Madame Vaele should say that nothing could be more natural. She had decided to use the ready-made language of politeness which took into consideration my reactions and didn't care about hers for, like now, the things she was saying were falsifying her. But I was glad she said what she had said. Otherwise it would have been a nasty business. She must have been very pretty some ten or fifteen years ago. She now looked weary and withering. But something of the past still remained; it always does. Her eyes remained beautiful.

'You know, madame? Not all people will think so,' I said.

'I know,' she smiled. 'We are all one. That God made some white, others black, others yellow, and others red hasn't the least importance. What is essential is understanding. Tell me, you have your parents?'

"But, *maman*, I told you,' said Thérèse petulantly.

'Yes, *ma chérie*' her mother said.

'Then why do you ask again?'

'I want him to tell me himself.'

'*Bon*,' Thérèse shrugged her shoulders and looked away. Bibi was smiling.

But Thérèse should have realized that it wasn't easy for her mother. It was because of her that her mother was there, not because of me. If she had come it was because she loved Thérèse. It was unfair to be ungrateful.

'Yes, madame,' I said. 'I have my parents, but they are far away.'

'You miss them?'

'Only when Thérèse keeps on singing your name. Everything: "I shall tell *maman*." Everything: "I shall tell *maman*!" *I* want to be able to say the same,' I laughed. 'But I can't. I'd have to write and it would take more than a week for my mother to receive my complaint; another week, perhaps two, for her to reply. And of course she would never come here and warn Thérèse that she has to be nice, that it isn't easy bringing up a son—'

'It's not easy at all; that I know. It's the same thing with a daughter.'

I understood her. My humour had misfired. But I tried again. What I wanted was to lighten the atmosphere, to make things easy for her, for Thérèse, for myself, and why not? For Bibi.

'It's true,' I went on. 'If my mother came here she would warn Thérèse to be careful, that once a son had been brought up, people shouldn't treat him anyhow.'

'Because Thérèse treats you anyhow?'

'*Si*. She's very wicked.'

'It doesn't please me to hear that.'

'Well caught!' Thérèse said in an undertone.

'But it's true,' I said to her mother. 'And yet I treat her like a princess.'

'That's not true,' Thérèse protested. 'That's not true!'

'Ask Bibi,' I said.

Bibi burst out laughing.

'So it's not true?' Madame Vaele asked. 'Eh, Bibi?'

'Not at all,' Bibi said. 'He's the most wicked man on earth. You don't know him.'

'He doesn't look wicked to me,' Madame Vaele said, smiling.

'That's how they are,' I said. 'Bibi and Thérèse have one head, one mouth, one heart. They're like one person.'

The lady liked that. She looked at Bibi gratefully for I must have confirmed what she was already thinking about the two girls. And Thérèse hadn't other girl friends. In fact, as she herself used to tell me, she hadn't had friends until Bibi came to their house. She was her only friend, beside me. Laurent had also been a friend. But he wasn't any longer. In her world Thérèse had only her parents with whom she had tense relations, and then Bibi and me. That must have been the reason why her mother appreciated Bibi's reported devotion to her daughter. A woman always wants her daughter to be happy and friends are a source of happiness, especially when they are girl friends. When there are boys around, advice and warnings are necessary and it strains the relations between mother and daughter. Madame Vaele was very glad about what I had just said. Bibi and Thérèse were one person, one head, one heart, one mouth …

'It's normal, no?' Thérèse said. 'It's normal that we should be like one person, no?'

'I didn't say the contrary,' I said. 'But it's not because of that that you no longer speak the truth. You are wicked, and you know it. Madame it's true. Sometimes I feel tempted to beat her up—'

'Never!' Madame Vaele said. 'A woman must never be beaten. It's not done.'

The waiter returned with the coffee and fruit juice on his tray.

'It's done back home, in Africa,' I said.

'But we're not in Africa,' Bibi said.

The waiter, putting the cups of coffee on the table, smiled. 'We're in France,' he said.

'*Voila!*' Thérèse snapped. 'But he won't accept it. His favourite argument is that he is like the tortoise. He travels with his home.'

The waiter, opening the bottle of fruit juice, roared with laughter. Madame Vaele also laughed.

'That's a good one,' the waiter laughed, putting the bottle on the table.

He was still laughing as he strode back to the counter. He was apparently pleased with what he had heard. It was exotic, refreshing, something to remember to repeat at table to his wife. A nice little story to tell. She too would laugh.

'It's funny,' I said. 'In Africa people wouldn't laugh at such a remark. It's a proverb. It's wisdom. You don't laugh at wisdom. It makes you think. That's how it is in Africa.'

'How many times must you be told that this isn't Africa?' Bibi asked, with mock severity. 'How many times?'

She was joking with me. That was the first time. No. It began that night at the dance. Before that she had some kind of reserve. Either she wanted me to respect her or she respected me. It seemed as though I intimidated her until that night at the dance. I don't know what came over her when she suddenly decided to stare fixedly into my eyes through the smoke of her cigarette. No; I know what made her do that. How could I have said I didn't know? It was because of Laurent, that dance he had with Thérèse. But why could that one dance have made her so jealous as to want to revenge herself? Laurent had danced with Thérèse before, on other occasions. I had danced with Bibi. Could she then have intercepted that look, the one I also saw? Laurent had overdone it, making eyes at Thérèse like that. Perhaps that was what made the difference. Bibi must have noticed it. And then I talked of jealousy. Perhaps that was what put the idea into her head. She may not have cared. But why did Thérèse hesitate? Why had she hesitated when Laurent asked her to dance? Had she noticed that I had caught Laurent making eyes at her? Well, no matter what reasons motivated our actions that night, the fact remained that that was when Bibi really became direct with me. Her reserve gave way. Now she was talking to me as she would have talked to Laurent, scoldingly. After that afternoon during which I betrayed Thérèse and she betrayed Laurent, we had held two more sessions and Bibi had talked freely about Thérèse and about her parents. We had become fond of each other. So, after all, she had the right to talk to me the way she was now talking to me. Only I wondered whether Thérèse hadn't noticed the slight change in Bibi's attitude towards me.

Chapter Five

'Look at your room,' Thérèse said as soon as she sat down on the bed. 'Look! Didn't the good lady make it?'

'It's my fault,' I said, sitting down. 'She was going to make it. It's I who said she shouldn't bother. I slept late and was still sleepy when she knocked on the door.'

'You slept late?'

'Yes.'

'When did you go to bed?'

'Midnight. No. Later than that.'

'What were you doing?'

'Writing.'

On returning from that interview with her mother the previous day I had come home and had sat at the type-writer. I wanted to write a novel about Laurent and Bibi, Thérèse and her mother and the shadow of her father; all that built around my involvement first with Thérèse and then with Bibi, and the possible repercussions on Laurent and Monsieur and Madame Vaele.

I had typed one page after another. They were all unsatisfactory. I would crumple up a page I had just finished typing and throw it on the floor. Then I would begin another, only to crumple it up. I wasn't getting down on paper what I really wanted.

It was those crumpled up pages that gave the room the shabby aspect Thérèse was complaining about. I had worked until ten and had eaten only a little bread and marmalade. For the first time I was beginning to take writing seriously. Perhaps that was why I became so fastidious. However, at ten, since it would have disturbed Madame Bistrott, the landlady, had I continued to type, I stopped work and went to bed.

'No. I went to bed at ten. But I couldn't sleep.'

'Why?'

'I don't know. I was thinking of the story I want to write. I want it to end happily—'

'That's writing for children.'

'Why?'

'Who still believes in all those reconciliations, those fanfares at the end of dramas. Only children who still have their fairylands. Listen, if you want to write, write something tragic. *Au fond* all life is tragic. To say the contrary is to lie.'

'Courage, Thérèse. Courage.'

'I haven't got it.'

Tomorrow, or the day after tomorrow, she would lean her head against my chest and say I had taught her to hope, that she was hoping, that she didn't know what she would do when I decided to leave her. She always said she knew I would leave her, what with all those pretty girls around, slim, cute, coquettish? Thérèse! It does something to a man to hear all that, especially when he is the woman's first man. One feels a kind of attachment, a kind of responsibility; and one wants things to end well for the woman.

The previous night I had tried to sleep. But sleep wouldn't come. I wondered what Laurent would do when he came to know what was happening. And Thérèse? What would she do? And her father? It was true that they said he loved Africa. But I suspected that that was because he had a firm there. Thérèse even said he loved Africans. I didn't like that. Africans weren't begging to be loved. If someone wanted to love Africans, he had to begin by loving humanity in general. To pick on Africans and say one loved them had something condescending about it that I found repulsive. But it was different with the sort of love I knew Thérèse had for Africa. She loved Africa through me. That was different. One can understand passion. It engages the whole spiritual horizon in a way that makes insincerity impossible. One can't say the same for that arm-chair love many people paraded all over Europe and America. Much of it was precocious and opportunistic.

Sleep had simply refused to come to me. I had thought and thought. 1 would have taken sleeping pills that night had there been any in the house. I wondered what her father would think, what he would say, what he would do, when he knew that an African was between him and the young French boy who could become his son-in-law.

As I lay there, on the bed, I was conscious of a conflict

developing in me, a conflict between the imagination and the events which had so far resulted from my relations with the people I wanted to portray. I wanted to write a novel and not autobiography. But the situation in which Thérèse and Bibi had put me was such that I felt more inclined to write about it than to invent events in the workshop of the imagination. But what end should I give to the story? That wasn't easy.

Sleep only came when I decided I would suspend thinking about the novel until after two months or three. I had to wait and see how things would work themselves out before writing about that spring and summer.

My studies at the faculty were suffering. I had given up the examinations. I hoped to take them in autumn.

'Where's the broom?' Thérèse asked.

'Don't worry, Thérèse. Madame Bistrott will make the room tomorrow.'

'No. I'm going to do it. It hurts my eyes to see your place like this. Paper everywhere. Is it the Laurent contagion or what?'

'No, my dear,' I said. 'His case is different.'

She began to pick up the crumpled typing sheets. She put them in a plastic waste paper basket.

When she had finished picking up the papers, she asked again for the broom. 'I can't leave the room like this,' she said.

'I've told you not to bother,' I said. 'Madame Bistrott would be furious. She wants to clean the house herself …'

Madame Bistrott was seventy-seven years old. One day I told her that she already had enough work cleaning the rest of the house. I could therefore help her with my room.

'What do you mean by that, monsieur?' she had asked. 'I am still solid you know. I've always cleaned the whole house myself. It's nothing; I'm going to do it as I have the habit of doing.'

She was very kind, especially as she allowed me to receive visitors, even at night. My friends could stay the night if they wished. She didn't mind. She once said she wasn't an old girl. She knew what life was; and, she had pointed out, youth was brief. One must take advantage of it.

Monsieur Bistrott had died five years prior to my arrival in the house. And whenever I conversed with Madame Bistrott over a cup of coffee in the sitting-room, it was to hear her talk about her husband's courage. She talked proudly about his *Médaille de Guerre*, a French military decoration.

Thérèse gave up the broom business. She sat down, on the bed.

'What impression did my mother make on you yesterday?' she asked, crossing her legs.

'It was funny—'

'Funny!'

'Yes. You know, with me sitting there and then your mother …'

'Et alors?'

'But listen, knowing that she knows …'

'But what can that do?'

'Since she's so Catholic. You said she's very pious—'

'Ah, that! But at her age you know …' 'She isn't very old, Thérèse. How old did you say she was?'

'Forty-five.'

'That's nothing. She's almost a girl.'

'Tu parles!'

'It's true. She's still young—'

'Was that the impression she gave?'

'Impression! No. She's young, she's young. That's all. As for the impression I think it was very favourable—'

'I can see it was …'

'I think she's an extremely nice person. It's true. But perhaps it's too early to judge.'

Thérèse rose and went to the window; and, looking out, she said:

'She gets on my nerves.'

I didn't like that. I am attached to my parents, very much. I am even attached to my ancestors whom I never knew. So I can't understand people being discourteous about their parents. In Africa the situation is a bit better; positively better. But in Europe, it is catastrophic, It was as if, acting from the other side of objective existence, children adopted men and women who then assumed, once the children were born, the official designation of parents. And once the children grew up, the work was done; they sacked the men and women who had been their parents, their employees.

In Africa the ties endure, they are blood ties that can't be broken without the people involved suffering for it. For, after all, children *are* their parents and to rebel against the man and woman who united to make the child possible is like rebelling against oneself. To hate them is like hating oneself.

'She gets on my nerves,' Thérèse had just said!

I talked to her often about my parents. I told her how I loved them, how they loved me. I said it was like that in Africa. There were a few differences of course. But parents and their children were one, from the beginning to the end. The family wasn't only husband and wife and their children. The family was many people. And yet there I was, in Paris, a cause of even more tension in the relationship between Thérèse and her parents. If she came to hate them, if she came to despise them, it would be because of me; and yet I would be the last person to allow any woman to make me despise my parents, not to speak of making me hate them.

Not that I deliberately wanted to foul her relationship with her parents. I couldn't do that. But the way things were developing made the paroxysm of their already tense relationship inevitable.

'Thérèse,' I said, 'do you love your parents?'

She turned away from the window and looking at me, she asked:

'Why do you ask?'

'It's because of the way you talk about your mother. Do you love them?'

She shrugged her shoulders. 'I don't know,' she said. 'They get on my nerves.'

That's one of the things that was good about her. She was honest. By saying she didn't know, she was making me understand that she didn't love them. To have said yes, I love my parents, very much, would have been a lie. And it's terrible to lie about one's heart. One could lie about things like the cinema, saying, for example, that one had gone to the cinema and talking about a film one had seen two days earlier, to hide the fact that one had gone dancing; but one can't lie about love, except if one is very dishonest. Thérèse wasn't dishonest. She was a plain, simple, pretty girl, who however was gaining some sort of confidence in herself, who was beginning to assert herself. And if she didn't love her parents it couldn't have been her fault. And I imagine it wasn't theirs either. They must have meant well in everything. I was sorry for her parents after what Thérèse had just said. But I was also sorry for her, because I knew she would have loved to love them. She had said she hadn't any courage!

A few weeks ago I had talked to her about Ewudu. But I didn't tell Thérèse how promiscuous Ewudu was. I talked to her about the Mungo River, about the love songs. But I played down the unfaithfulness of the men and women. I didn't want to put the idea in her head. I hate loose women, although I am myself a bit loose. That's funny, perhaps a bit unfair too. But it's like that. I didn't want Thérèse to be like Ewudu, so I didn't tell her everything. I know it was wrong not to have given her an objective picture of the Mungo River. But I also knew, and still know, that it would have been wrong to talk to her about the details of that voluptuousness. I had already gone too far with her. And there was no reason for corrupting her even more. But then, to have done so wouldn't have been in my interest. If Thérèse had heard about everything Ewudu did and then said, okay, if it is so, then I'd do the same, I would have dropped her immediately. I hate a woman who sleeps with men right and left. It's after all natural—I mean, that I should hate such women. The real trouble with me was that—and I am glad things are changing—I was very immoral; but still, when I talked, I could sincerely be very moralistic. But that was because I knew what was good and wanted people to know it, in case they didn't care. While I personally tried to do what was good, I only succeeded quite often in doing what many would term immoral. Besides Thérèse there was Ndome, a Cameroonian girl, with whom I was intimate; and now Bibi had also been brought in. I knew it was bad, wrong, 'immoral'. But I also knew it felt good, very pleasurable, doing with Ndome and Bibi, what I did with Thérèse. And yet I didn't want Thérèse to go with other boys. If only she knew! Thérèse! But perhaps it is out of such contradictions, out of such conflicts that art evolves, grows, manifests itself. To live the night and feel the day; to hate to love the things one loves.

From my room we went to the Latin Quarter.

Crowds of students. Crowds of non-students. We

walked up the Boulevard Saint Michel, had coffee at the counter of the café *Au Depart*, and then went into the Luxembourg Gardens.

Children played. They were with their mothers or the girls who took care of them. Some of the girls were foreign girls, like Bibi, who had come to Paris to learn French.

Thérèse and I sat close to each other on iron chairs. People held shiny faces to the sun.

I shouldn't fail the examinations in September, I thought. That would be the last chance of the year.

I didn't want to repeat the class. My parents were waiting for my results. Thérèse's parents were also waiting for hers, hoping she would pass. But like me, she too had decided to wait until the autumn session.

The wind folded the water in the basin of the fountain. The wind folded the water into little waves, giving the children, whose toy sailing boats cruised on it, a toy idea of the sea. But perhaps they couldn't appreciate the resemblance. Most of them may not have seen the sea; but many were bound to see it, in a matter of weeks. May was ending. The summer holidays weren't far away any longer; and many parents spent them by the sea.

It would be terrible if I failed the exams, in the autumn, I thought …

'Have you seen Laurent since?' Thérèse asked.

'No,' I said. 'I was thinking of going to his place one of these days.'

'Non!'

'Why?'

'I don't want him in our company any more.'

'And Bibi?'

'She can continue to see him if she likes. He's a filthy fellow.'

It was as if she had said it about me. Thérèse! If only she knew what was going on.

'Have you told your parents that you're not taking the exams,' I said, to change the subject.

'Ohpff,' she said. 'Why tell them? Papa would be furious.'

'But they'd know all the same. They'd ask you.'

'I shall tell them when they ask, but not before—'

'Won't they be furious?'

'But of course, especially my father.'

'Then why not tell them before they ask? You make them hope for nothing. They'd be so disappointed.'

'*Tant pis*. I'll wait for them to ask me. If I told them now, papa would want to force me to take them. I'm not prepared—'

'Your mother will blame it on me.'

'I don't see why?'

The leaves on the trees were a rich green. The leaves were compact after the tender sparceness of early spring. People strolled in twos or in threes. There were larger groups, chatting or chattering. Plenty of gaiety and laughter. But some strolled alone, silent and thoughtful, which was natural even though their solitude wasn't.

'You think your father would want to force you to take the exams?'

'Yes. He's like that. It's only he who is right.'

'And if you fail?'

'What won't he say?'

The children shouted and laughed—it's so funny, a child's laughter—and their hilarity was strident. They shouted and laughed, some cried, by the fountain where the wind gaily filled the sails of their toy boats.

A man walked a donkey. It drew a carriage. Children took turns in it. They waved to their mothers and nurses as the donkey passed. It was a fine afternoon.

'You know, I haven't been able to understand why Laurent did that? We can have our weaknesses, but it's not at all encouraging that others should be like us. Why should he have wanted to do that?'

'How do you expect me to know?'

'You think he meant what he said?'

'What makes you think he didn't mean it?'

'I don't know. I've simply been unable to understand why he would have behaved like that.'

'Because I am pretty.'

'Who told you you were pretty?'

'Laurent.'

'And it flattered you, didn't it?'

'Very much. Are you jealous?'

'Me, jealous?'

'Yes.'

'Of course,' I joked. 'That's why I want us to go to his place.'

'To do what?'

'To break his jaw!'

'True?'

'Of course!'

'No. It's not true. You're joking.'

'Me, joking?'

'Yes. See, the corner of your lip is twitching … Why are you laughing?'

'Who told you I am laughing?'

'I have eyes. See! Your lip is twitching. Why are you laughing? But, Doumbe, tell me, why aren't you jealous?'

'But I told you I am, very jealous.'

'It's not true. You're laughing, see, your lip … So I don't mean anything to you?'

'Oh, no, my dear! Thérèse you know you are a sprig of green leaves and flowers, eternal charm. You're more exquisite than art, more endearing than the most tender of dreams. Thérèse you know that.'

'It's your tongue that says so. But your heart?'

I shrugged, laughed and stroked her hair. 'It's frustrating, don't you think?' I said. 'Why was it hidden? If the heart were like the eyes, one could read it. But it's not. Anyway you must trust me. You must believe what I say. You must know that what my tongue says my heart sings, in its depths.'

'Sings what?'

'What I said just now about you …'
'But what?'
'But you heard me say it, Thérèse.'
'Say it again.'
'Why, you heard it, didn't you?'
'Yes.'
'Well then?'
'But repeat it all the same.'
'I've forgotten it,' I smiled.
She too smiled, gloomily, and said:
'Because it didn't come from your heart.'
I stroked her hair.

An old lady walked up to us. She was thin and her cheeks were sunken. She licked her fingers and cut two tickets from a book of tickets she held in her trembling left hand. She handed me the tickets.

Children were shouting joyously at the fountain. The donkey and the carriage and the children. The toy sailing boats on the water. The children were laughing in advance their laughter of years to come.

My hand was in my pocket feeling for a franc to give the old lady. She didn't look resigned. It didn't look as though she had laughed lately, nor did it seem she would laugh again. She had outlived laughter. Perhaps she had been widowed by the war, a terrible thing.

I gave the old lady a franc and she moved away, shuffling towards a couple on our right, a few chairs away. The girl's eyes were closed, her head thrown backwards, her face which was oily and shiny was surrendered to the sky and its fiery sun. The boy was reading a newspaper in spite of the sun.

As the ticket woman approached, the boy looked up from his newspaper. The girl didn't move. She had very long, beautiful legs.

The children shouted by the fountain.

The donkey with its carriage in which children laughed and waved passed, raising a little dust. The man who walked it led the animal round and round the fountain.

'I still don't understand Bibi, you know,' I said, 'I mean about Laurent. What does she see in him?'

'Oh pff,' Thérèse shrugged, frowning. 'She's nice, that's all. Too nice I'd say. A boy who has no money and won't work, and still she thinks of no one else but him. Now her big idea is to find work as soon as her French is better. She wants to help him because he's an artist.'

'You make it sound as though they were already married and he was a lazy husband being supported by his wife.'

'But that is how he will end, Laurent. He'll never be able to earn a living.'

'He'll paint.'

'Paint?'

'Why not?'

'It doesn't pay.'

'Why? If he has the talent, and maybe if he's launched.'

'Who will launch him? Bibi?'

'Why only Bibi?'

'Because he hasn't anyone else. Bibi is all he has, and Bibi has nothing.'

'And if he loses her?'

'He'll find another girl. But certainly not one who would be prepared to do what Bibi does for him. I can assure you she thinks of no one else but him. It's incredible. Sometimes I have the impression she wants him to marry her—'

'You said he's not in love with her.'

'But for an opportunist what difference does it make, love or no love?'

'You also said Bibi isn't in love with him either.'

'It's true. It's easy to tell when a woman is in love with a man.'

'Then why does she think only of him?'

'She's obsessed, that's all, poor girl.'

'She may be fooling you.'

'Why should she fool me?'

'Because since we are together it would be nice for her to give the impression that she cares very much for him.'

'That's not true. She cares, sincerely.'

'Then she loves him.'

'Perhaps. Why not? But he's not worthy of being loved.'

'It's people like that who are loved you know. Not only Bibi. Marc also. I wonder what will happen when he returns from the army.'

'I think Laurent will drop Bibi.'

'But he can't be with Marc any more. You told me that Bibi said he's changed.'

'I don't think so. Bibi is naïve in spite of everything. Laurent may have said that only to make her feel she had accomplished the impossible. Who knows whether that is one of the reasons of her attachment to him? Change! *Tu parles!* You haven't noticed the way he looks at you?'

'No. How does he look at me?'

'He narrows his eyes and stares from behind his sly sockets and then he will sigh. I used to watch him.'

'I think we both have too much imagination.'

'Perhaps …'

The children laughed and shouted and some cried. The sun was shifting westwards, going to set.

'Let's talk about ourselves for a while,' I said.

'You think we're sufficiently interesting?' Thérèse asked.

'Yes.'

'You don't behave as though we were.'

'Why?'

'We spend whole hours talking about Bibi and Laurent …'

'It doesn't matter. Look at those children.'

'What about them?'

'How would you like to have one?'

'One of those?'

'No. One we'd make ourselves.'

'When?'

'One of these days—'

'Are you mad, *non*?'

'Why?'
'And besides, it's impossible.'
'How is it impossible?'
'Because I'm not pregnant.'
'Should I decide to—'
'Decide to do what?'
'You know what I mean.'
'*Pas question*. You'll keep your *waist-coat* on.'
'And if I refuse?'
'Then you can go and look for someone else.'

I didn't like it when she talked like that, and she had recently been talking that way more and more frequently. The humble Thérèse was no more. It was another one, snappy, even bold, who had taken her place. But something of the former Thérèse remained in the girl who was sitting with me in the Luxembourg Gardens that afternoon.

After a long silence I said:

'Why did you say that?'

'What?'

'That I'd have to go and look for someone else. You know it hurts me? If I spoke of a child it was because I felt I'd love to have a child by you. Why can't you understand that?'

'I do understand,' she said, her attitude softening. 'But I just don't want a child now. It would kill me. Later perhaps. But now, Doumbe, no. Be reasonable.'

She took one of my hands and squeezed it tenderly.

'Later,' I mused.

'Yes, Doumbe,' Thérèse said. 'I'd love to have a child. It's true.'

'Then why not now?'

She ignored the question as she raised her face towards mine. Then she looked away and said:

'I'd love to have a child, you know. It would amuse me.' She turned her face and stared into my eyes, and I saw a sickly weariness come over her. She looked exhausted. 'No,' she breathed, shaking her head as if she were going to cry. 'We can't have it now. I have my parents and, Doumbe, we're only lovers.'

All that was true. But why did the fact make me feel so ashamed of myself? What was wrong or improper in our being only that—lovers? But there was Thérèse, at nineteen, her studies, like mine, drifting, the peace of her family at stake, because of me, and now she was complaining by implication that I made love to her out of wedlock!

There were many sailing boats on the water, children's toys, and there was a little wind. A nice fairy sea. The children shouted and laughed, some cried.

A shadow fell over us. The sun was getting wrapped up in the clouds as it slid to the horizon.

Chapter Six

O N the afternoon of the following Sunday Thérèse and I went to a *matinée* at the Moulin de Montparnasse, a dancehall which was next door to the *Bobino* in the Rue de la Gaîté.

We went in in high spirits and as we danced we felt more and more light-hearted, more and more happy. We had danced a cha-cha-cha and were now dancing a bolero, a beautiful dance; but it was ending.

The band rested; the crowd of dancers remained on the floor. The band didn't actually rest. It only switched, after a minute's pause, from the bolero to a rock. The crowds on the floor began to thin out, leaving the floor to lovers of quick dances. Thérèse said we should go and sit down. I had almost forgotten that her hips and buttocks were rather incongruous for jumpy dances like the rock. By saying that we should go and sit down she reminded me of the fact, and rather painfully, because I knew she liked dancing, even liked the rock; but she never brought herself to do it. She said it didn't go well with her. Once she had corrected herself with a touch of self-mockery when she had said it was she who didn't go well with the rock.

She was too heavy, she said. I told her that at home, in Africa, it was forbidden to talk of a man or woman, girl or boy, even of a child no matter what they were like as being heavy. She had shrugged her shoulders. So that afternoon again she said we shouldn't dance the rock.

We went and sat down. She sat opposite me and asked me if she didn't bore me. I said no, why, how could she bore me?

She smiled morosely. 'I'm ugly,' she said.

I looked away from her. The rock was really hot. Couples turned and jumped and tapped and whirled. The band was frantic. An African boy in a dark three piece suit—or perhaps a West Indian—danced with an extremely slim and pretty blonde. They danced beautifully.

After the rock people began to return to their seats.

'She's very pretty, eh?' Thérèse observed.

'Who?' I asked.

'The blonde.'

'Oh, yes,' I said, innocently.

The effect was immediate and tragic.

Thérèse sat back in her chair, deflated and humiliated.

I reached out for her hand, and took it in mine.

The band began to play a tango.

'Let's dance,' I said.

She shook her head. I saw tears in her eyes.

'Thérèse!' I breathed, leaning forward. 'You know you aren't ugly.'

'But do you love me?'

What I could have called love then were those moody moments when I felt alone, even when she was there, by my side. Moments of melancholy when the world seemed a silent place waiting for the few voices that could still articulate the life-words that recall hope when the distance begins to woo it. But those moody moments never lasted. What persisted was the fondness and that was all I could declare to Thérèse, now; but I knew she wanted more than that. She needed love.

'Thérèse!'

'Est-ce que tu m'aimes?'

'Let your heart tell you what lies beyond words,' I said, taking refuge in the abstract.

'Do you love me?' she repeated and the tears began to run down her cheeks.

The vocalist in the band began to sing in Spanish.

Thérèse. She took her handbag with her right hand. I didn't let go of her left hand which was in my right. So I too rose. She put her handbag on the table, opened it with one hand, took a handkerchief from it and wiped her eyes. She shut the handbag without having replaced the handkerchief in it.

She sighed and looked at me.

'Let's go,' she said.

People were happy on the dance-floor. And that, in spite of the melancholy of the tango. Slim girls whose faces weren't prettier than Thérèse's; but who were slim as Thérèse would have liked to be.

The few couples who weren't dancing stared at us. Some didn't. I led Thérèse to the exit.

May ended. I continued to be unfaithful to Thérèse. That was mainly because of Bibi. Somehow it seemed to me as though our hearts didn't care; but our bodies did, very much. At least mine did. But there may not even be any difference between the body and the heart.

Bibi and I enjoyed our secret pleasures. We kept on telling each other that we should guard against Thérèse or Laurent finding out anything about what was going on behind their backs. We had to be careful. We weren't the only people who betrayed their friends in that manner.

'You said you don't hide anything from each other,' I once remarked.

She smiled. 'It depends,' she said. 'I'm not a child. But I know Thérèse doesn't hide anything from me.'

'If we are as loose upstairs as we are downstairs, Thérèse and Laurent would know about us tomorrow.'

Bibi gave me a light tap on my cheek with the tips of her fingers. 'I'm not loose downstairs,' she said. 'I don't think I am. Do you find me loose?'

'You're all right, tight,' I said.

'Then I am also tight-lipped,' she said. 'So you see I won't talk. And you?'

'I don't know.'

'How's that?'

'But, Bibi, I can neither be tight nor loose. I'm not made like you.'

She smiled. 'You're long-tongued,' she said. 'So it's you who would talk.'

'I don't like the comparison,' I protested. 'I don't like that image.'

'Why?'

'I'm not French ... Does Laurent use his tongue?'

'Of course. He isn't dumb—'

'Come on. I didn't mean that. I didn't mean in speaking ...'

After Thérèse and Bibi, there was Ndome. But with her it was a return. I became involved with the three of them. It was risky. But I was going to write. I had to live, and the pleasure which women gave, their life, was the very depth of existence. I liked women. I shall write and immortalize their names: Thérèse, Bibi, Ndome, and those who had been before them, and those who will come after.

I was in my room one afternoon when the doorbell rang. But before I could get to the corridor Madame Bistrott had gone to the door. I heard her turn the key as I was opening the door of my room. Ndome thanked Madame Bistrott and walked towards me. Ndom'a Munjamwasu. She knew one of my aunts in Duala. Her parents were friends of my aunt.

The last time Ndome had visited me was three weeks ago.

Behind her Madame Bistrott was locking the door. I waited for the lady to raise her head so that I could thank her. She looked in my direction, expecting to be thanked.

'*Merci, madame,*' I said.

She nodded, and her eyes narrowed connivingly, almost roguishly. She was such an understanding old woman. If it had been someone else—an old girl for example—I wouldn't have lived in that room for a week. I'd have been turned out. But that doesn't mean I received women very often. After all I had my studies, and my short stories and poems to write. But students were turned out of their rooms because of a single visit—a feminine visit. Some weren't even allowed to receive boys. Visits were forbidden. But not so at Madame Bistrott's, kind old lady.

Ndome, slender, pretty, attractive, in a print dress over which she wore a loin-cloth, was lightly perfumed. She had a headscarf on her stretched hair. The headscarf was raised at the back, which, with her dress and the loin-cloth and the smooth brown of her complexion, made her look like the women of Northern Cameroon.

The last time she visited me three weeks ago she had refused to be nice—you know what I mean—and had said she had found a fiancé or a fiancé had found her. I don't know which! They were going to get married, she had said. She had handed the keys of her body to him, and all that.

'*Ingea*,' I said in Duala.

She came in and I shut the door.

It was around four in the afternoon. Ndome went to the window and leaned out; but only for a few seconds.

She turned round and in mock disgust, she said:

'Look at your adulterous eyes.'

'What is wrong with them?' I asked.

'Nothing ... Doumbe, I'm hungry.'

'Haven't you eaten?'

'I arrived late at the restaurant.'

She meant the university restaurant. She was a student.

'You could have gone to a self-service.'

'Why, because there's nothing in the house?'

'There's some fried chicken and butter and bread.'

'Bring them, quick.'

'Look in the sideboard.'

She opened the sideboard in which I kept drinks and other provisions—sugar, tea, coffee, biscuits and so on—for my guests; and myself when I wanted a quick bite or felt like having a cup of coffee and didn't want to go out to the café round the corner.

Ndome took off her headscarf and flung in on the bed. Then she returned to the sideboard and brought out the plate on which the chicken was. She put it on the table. Then she took the bread. She sat down to eat. Just then, the door-bell rang.

I quickly opened the door and hurried down the corridor. I didn't want the old lady to get up again. I knew the visit was for me. Madame Bistrott rarely had visitors of her own.

I opened the main door and there was Thérèse. I didn't kiss her.

'*Tiens!*' I said. 'I wasn't expecting you.'

'I know,' she said and raised her right foot from the

doormat and placed her handbag on her thigh. 'I came to give you an invitation.'

'What's it about?'

'A friend of my father's is speaking tonight. He's the Ambassador of the Ivory Coast.'

She handed me the invitation and then replaced her foot on the doormat and shut her handbag.

I read the invitation.

'Does it interest you?' Thérèse asked.

'Of course. But why didn't you tell me earlier?'

'It was only yesterday afternoon that we received the invitations.'

'Will your parents be there?'

'Yes.'

'It would be an opportunity for me to meet your father.'

'Yes, if you want.'

'But I doubt if I'll be able to make it. However we shall see. Come in.'

She smiled pathetically. 'It was beginning to get disturbing,' she said.

'What?'

She stepped into the corridor and I shut the door and turned the key.

'That I was being received on the landing,' she said.

I put my hand on her shoulder and gently urged her forward. I didn't want us to be chatting in the corridor. Too much noise. The old lady was nice and kind; but I had nevertheless to be careful.

'Thérèse,' I said, introducing the two girls, 'Ndome, a compatriot.'

Thérèse went forward. But it was as if the African girl wasn't seeing her. She was unmoved. Then when she belatedly looked up, she did so with a lot of contempt showing on her face. She held out her arm, a piece of bread in her hand, her fingers greasy.

Thérèse didn't seem to know what to do with Ndome's arm; but after a moment's indecision she understood. She touched the arm with her fingers. Ndome didn't say she was happy to make her acquaintance. Thérèse looked at me shyly as Ndome returned her eyes to her plate.

'That's being impolite,' I said, in Duala. 'Ndome, I hate such manners.'

Thérèse sat down.

Ndome looked at me, then she burst out laughing.

'Look at him,' she cried, in Duala. 'He's annoyed, siding with his wife.' Calling Thérèse my wife was of course being ironical. 'Look at him!' Then she stopped laughing and glancing at Thérèse who was flushing, embarrassed, Ndome said: '*Mbè boso!*'

'What is wrong with her face?' I asked in Duala.

'Nothing,' Ndome replied. 'Everyone with his own. Ekwe carried that shit; now you have carried I don't know what.'

Ekwe Milongi was a Cameroonian agronomist who was married to a French girl. She was expecting their first child. Ndome said the girl wasn't hospitable. I rarely went to their place. Ndome complained that it was the girl who ruled the house. Ekwe did her bidding. It shocked Ndome very much that a woman should lord it over a man. I didn't like it either.

And now she was criticizing Thérèse's looks, her face.

But although Thérèse would have agreed with Ndome had she heard what we were saying in Duala, I didn't think Thérèse was ugly. I loved her face. The simple, intimate eyes.

'Leave her alone,' I said.

'Look at her neck!' Ndome mocked, not looking at Thérèse.

'It's a crane's neck,' I laughed. 'A swan's neck.'

'Would you marry her?'

'*Na!* You haven't any other thing in that big head of yours but marriage?'

Her head wasn't big.

Thérèse looked first at Ndome, then at me. Then she asked:

'What are you two saying?'

'It's our language,' Ndome said in French, wickedly. '*C'est notre langue.* If you don't understand it that's your business. It isn't our fault. *Je regrette.*'

This silenced Thérèse. In order to cheer her up I began to talk of the Centre where, according to the invitation, the Ivory Coast Ambassador was going to speak that evening on *The Industrialization of Africa*.

'I know some people at the centre,' I said. 'Last time

it was something about South Africa. It was an African Nationalist leader who spoke.'

'Bon?'

'Yes.'

Ndome licked her fingers.

'I am eating with my fingers,' she said, in Duala. 'Kill yourself, white woman, if you want. That's how my grandmother ate. She lived to be eighty.'

Ndome got up.

'What's there to drink?' she asked.

'Everything, from champagne to rain water,' I said.

She opened the sideboard. She looked from one corner to the other.

'I can see only a little whisky and a little water, that is mineral water.' She straightened up. 'You haven't any wine?'

'No.'

'How can one eat without a little wine?'

'Ndome, your grandmother didn't eat with wine. She lived to be eighty.'

'I know,' she said. 'It's the useless white people who have taught me to drink it. What can I do?'

'You can refuse to drink it …'

'Tomorrow,' she said. 'I've finished the chicken.'

'I can see you have, and the bread.'

'Are you angry?'

'Yes. I've never been so angry before.'

'Knock your head against that wall to prove that you

are angry ... If I don't eat now when will I eat again? Soon your white wife will block the door like Ekwe's. *Aye*, that one!'

'I like your language,' said Thérèse innocently.

'How stupid!' Ndome said in Duala. 'You are being abused in that language and yet you like it all the same.'

'It's very musical,' I said, to Thérèse.

'It sounds like Italian,' she said.

'That I don't know,' I yawned. 'But it's like Lingala, the Congolese language.'

'Don't know ...'

'How would you?' Ndome blurted out, always in Duala.

She was leaning against the sideboard. She had a very pretty face, but a heart bitter against white girls. Every black boy who married a white girl meant a fiancé less for the marriage-conscious African girls.

'Leave her alone,' I said.

'I'm not holding her.' Ndome pouted; then she asked: 'Is the kitchen open?'

'Yes.'

'I'm going to wash my hands.'

She went to the kitchen.

'She's very pretty,' Thérèse observed honestly.

'She isn't bad,' I said.

'I have the impression she doesn't like me.'

'Do you like her?'

She shrugged, looked at me, then said, with a little smile:

'As a matter of fact I don't know.'

Ndome returned to the room.

Thérèse got up in her turn.

'Are you leaving?' Ndome asked her in French, then she added in Duala: 'Look at your face.'

'No,' Thérèse said and went out of the room.

I heard her open the door of the toilette. I thought she had gone there only to show Ndome that she wasn't a stranger in the house. Women do that at times.

The sun was still outside, on the walls. A high sky and it was blue.

That June was a lovely month; I was going to say a month of love.

'What useless hips!' Ndome cried in Duala. 'What mud!'

Thérèse had just entered and was going towards the bed. She sat down.

'Ndome, won't you shut up?'

'Doumbe, what do you do with such hips?'

Luckily Thérèse didn't understand Duala. There would have been tears.

But Ndome was only being traditional. We tended to mock at people rather than praise them. Flattery is rare, or was rare with us, since the old ways are dying away. I am against the whole-sale rejection of the past. With the Dualas and the Mongos, as well as with most of the coastal tribes of Cameroon, it was more usual to point out what was ugly about a man or woman than what was attractive about them. You saw a girl and when you talked about her to her boy friend, for example, you didn't say what a pretty girl! You said what shit!

You saw a child with its mother. Even if the child was handsome you told the mother that her child was ugly. What a head! Look at the eyes! Look at the face! The mother only smiled or laughed and told you that it didn't matter; that it was her child and let it be as it was.

But in Europe, or rather in France, you had to flatter, even if there was no reason to praise a woman's looks. To think that I did that sometimes! You even flattered babies; that is, you flattered the parents through their children. In fact, after being shown a child if you didn't say how handsome it was, the mother would herself say it. 'It's handsome, isn't it?' she would ask; naturally you would say yes. And she would kiss the poor child.

So what Ndome was saying was quite normal. But Thérèse was of another culture, and somehow I felt it was unfair to talk about her from the point of view of our own culture. It sounded cruel, like some Europeans who try to judge Africans from the European point of view as if things were as easy as that. I recall a friend who carried the story that I didn't like women! Simply because I thought a man didn't have to fawn upon a woman.

'Ndome,' I said, 'that's my own.'

'She's all hips and buttocks.'

But I had to put an end to that mockery.

'If you don't shut up it will end badly,' I warned.

My voice had an edge to it.

'You won't begin beating up your sister because of a white woman,' Ndome retorted. 'I said she has loaded hips—mud—and you want to swallow me.'

'Ndome!'

She saw that I was going to lose my temper.

'Don't be annoyed, papa,' she said, placatingly. 'Your wife is an angel.'

Of course she didn't mean it. Thérèse wasn't an angel. And happily she wasn't. She would have been a myth. She was a French girl, nineteen; the only daughter of Monsieur Jacques Vaele, a Parisian businessman with a firm in the Ivory Coast.

She wasn't a myth.

Thérèse got up.

'I'm going,' she said, reaching for her handbag.

'No. Why? Stay,' I said. 'Stay.'

'No. I have to be home before five. I have some shopping to do with my mother.'

'Okay. Do I see you on Monday? Three o'clock.'

'If you want … Won't you come tonight to the lecture?'

'I don't think so. However, I'll see …'

She shook Ndome's hand.

I walked with her down the corridor and then opened the door for her. She went out. I also went out and drew the door to behind me, without however shutting it completely.

We stood on the landing, facing each other. Her head was slightly tilted backwards and I looked into her eyes.

'Is she the girl you said you used to see before we met?' she asked, humbly.

'Yes,' I replied. 'But it's over.'

'Sure?'

'Yes.'

'*Sûr, sûr?*'

'Yes, Thérèse.'

She dropped her face, and said, doubtfully:

'I'm leaving you with her, Doumbe. Promise me …' She looked up. 'Promise …'

Her face lit up.

'You'd do nothing with her,' she said. 'Nothing.'

'Yes, Thérèse, believe me, nothing.'

Chapter Seven

But desire doesn't keep promises.

And Ndome had a practical tongue, an uninhibited, passionately vulgar tongue. But I say vulgar only because I lack another word.

'There you are,' she taunted me, as soon as I returned to the room. 'You're sad as if she won't return.'

'Who told you I'm sad?'

'Haven't I eyes? I don't know what you people see in those white girls. How are their things?'

'Wonderful.'

'*Na!* Oh, how intelligent you're being, talking about women! That's what they sent you to study.'

I went to her, seized her hand, twisted her arm and she cried. As if the pain was impossible to bare, she fell, naturally, on the bed. Ndome!

I fell on her, not exactly with the intention of doing anything intimate. No. I was only playing with her. It's so agreeable playing with a lively woman. But Ndome began to insinuate, to provoke me.

'What are you doing on me? Are you tired of your white woman's thing?'

'Shut up.'

'Shut up!' she mimicked. 'Look at your adulterous eyes! You're not tired of women.' She pushed me. 'You'll rumple my dress …'

'No, I won't.'

'I say you'll rumple it. Get up. Let me take it off.'

Ndome was in my room all afternoon. In the evening she went to the grocery on the ground-floor and bought rice. She bought other things. She also bought meat from the butcher. She spent over twenty francs. I wanted to refund her half the cost of everything she had bought. She laughed at me and said I was becoming like white people.

She prepared dinner for us, while I read a novel I had bought the previous day. When the food was ready, we ate and then night fell. We talked about home with a certain nostalgia, and I saw the past in my imagination. I realized how far the way was. We went to bed early, but actually fell asleep only towards midnight, and then we rose very early, feeling warm, almost hot, and Ndome put her hand between my thighs … By the time the early summer sun threw light on the curtains, the whole room, as the expression with the Mongos and Dualas has it, was smelling of adultery … We had discussed Thérèse. Ndome said she couldn't understand why African boys wouldn't leave white women alone. I laughed.

We had a bath together; then she cooked our breakfast. We had it in the kitchen. Then Ndome left. Some thirty minutes later I felt very sleepy. I fell on the bed and slept; but only for a couple of hours. When I woke up I gazed at the sky from the bed. I felt that moody nervousness that makes me think and think. I was tired ... Thérèse. Why was I so unfaithful to her? I saw her face in my imagination. It remained an innocent face in spite of what I had taught her. I felt I was being very unreasonable. Then I began to pity her. It's strange how I mixed pity with love and how love was a mood which was associated with tiredness ... What did she expect of me? Why did she trust me so much? Why did she say she had learned to hope because of me? Why was she so attached to me? And then what about her friend?

Bibi!

Oh, Bibi ... She had Laurent.

Ndome?

She had her fiancé.

But Thérèse had only me and her parents; and something had happened between her parents and her, something which had disturbed her feelings for them,

When Thérèse came to visit me on Monday, at three, I took her in my arms as soon as I had locked the door. I kissed her in the corridor.

She was a bit startled. I had never behaved so fawningly to her before.

We went into my room. I asked her to sit down,

'You weren't at the lecture,' she said.

'I couldn't. Listen, Thérèse,' I proposed, 'we're going to get married and as soon as possible.'

She looked at me, as if alarmed.

'But it's impossible,' she breathed. 'Or are you joking?'

'No,' I said, morosely. 'You'll be my wife. It's true. I can't wait any longer.'

Tears came to her eyes …

'It's impossible, Doumbe.'

'*Si*. It's possible.'

'But my parents?'

'They'd accept.'

'I don't think they would.'

'You mustn't be pessimistic. I think they'd accept. But first tell me. Are you in agreement?'

'Yes, Doumbe.'

And now she burst out, sobbing. She clung to my shoulder.

I waited.

When she calmed down, I mused:

'It's incredible how the past exiles itself in the memory.'

'Why do you say that?' she asked, wiping her eyes.

'I don't know,' I said, sincerely.

One week later I received a letter from Africa. It was from my father. He was recalling me home. He said my children would learn all the books. As for me, he thought I should be near him. He wasn't young any longer.

Although a Mongo, my father wrote in Duala. He said his father, my grandfather, had told him many things about the family and the land. Those things were our honour. They could never be the past. They were the present and the future for he was still alive and they were alive in him. But could he say how long he still had to live? my father asked in his letter. No. No one could say. And he wouldn't want to die without having talked to me about those things his father, my grandfather, told him before he died. There was a lot of work to be done. He was feeling he couldn't continue to do it alone. I'd have to come home and be by his side. So he was expecting me by the end of July. He would arrange for money to be sent to me. Someone would go to Tiko to transfer 'a few pennies' to me. I should come by air. He hoped the year's studies were ending well. My mother sent her greetings. She was well. Greetings from everybody …

That meant the end of my hopes for a civil service career. Not that I particularly wanted to work in the administration. I hadn't the temperament. I wanted to be a lawyer and write. But should my studies not give the results I was expecting I'd have to do something. So perhaps the civil service would finally be the solution. Of course I could refuse to join the civil service and go home and work on the land. But since I proposed to Thérèse a week ago I had revised my plans. A white woman on the land in Equatorial Africa, in village life, that seemed rather rough. I could stand it. My people were standing it. But Thérèse certainly wouldn't be able to stand it. So I had decided that if the hopes of becoming a lawyer didn't work out, I'd join the civil service. That would provide Thérèse with enough comfort in which to bring up our children. But my father's letter destroyed that dream. I decided to be calm and not rush with the news to Thérèse. I'd prepare her for it. I'd explain that she would get used to the village.

The letter arrived in the morning. In the afternoon, Bibi came to my place.

'How's Thérèse?' I asked as soon as Bibi had sat down.

'She's having a terrible day. She's locked herself up in her room.'

'Why?'

'It began last night. She told her father about you.'

'Yes?'

Bibi shook her head. 'It was terrible,' she said. 'Her father wanted to know if she had known you for a long time. And Thérèse said everything or nearly everything. You've been seeing each other for over three months. You're going to get married—'

'How did he take it?'

'He got very upset. And what made things worse was that only two days ago he learnt that Thérèse isn't taking the exams. And then last night, to hear about you! What didn't he say?'

'I suspected he wouldn't have it. But I thought perhaps …'

'You should have heard him last night. Thérèse had betrayed him, he said she was a prostitute. Yes, she must have slept with you, he cried at the top of his voice. Madame burst out crying and believe me, it was terrible to see.'

'What did he say about the marriage?'

'Nothing definite yet. He didn't refer to it directly.

The whole of last night it was tearing up Thérèse's character. He ended up on a note of despair. You should have seen him, elbows on the table, head in his hands, and then saying what an unfortunate man he was and all that …'

'Naturally … What did Thérèse say?'

'What can Thérèse say? It's only when she's with us that she talks a bit. At home she's completely closed up. With Madame also she can talk; but with her father—'

'You think they'll finally consent?'

'How should I know?'

'From the things he said last night.'

'No.'

'No?'

'He won't have it. I know monsieur.'

'And you?'

'What has it got to do with me?'

'Aren't you against my marrying Thérèse?'

'Why should I be? In fact, I've been expecting it for a long time. I knew you would want to marry her.'

'Why?'

'Men like a woman who thinks of herself as being very unfortunate. And then Thérèse is serious, faithful, obedient …'

'It would be amusing if Laurent followed our example. I mean if you two followed our example. We could get married on the same day, the four of us. It would be a reconciliation. You know Thérèse doesn't want us to have anything to do with you two when you are together, because of Laurent.'

'She told me.'

Bibi was perspiring under the armpits. Her face which had been more or less anxious a few moments ago was becoming relaxed.

The room was very clear with the light-hearted clarity of summer.

Bibi stretched her hands behind her, pinning them in the bedclothes. She leaned backwards.

The door-bell rang.

She sat up.

'You think it's Thérèse?' she asked.

'It's possible,' I said. 'I'm coming.'

As I turned to go to the corridor Bibi seized my hand. I stopped and we faced each other. She held those large eyes fixedly on me and she didn't look very happy. I wasn't feeling happy either.

The door-bell rang again.

'Let me go,' I said. I shook off her hand and turned towards the door; but she got up and held on to my shoulder and said:

'Listen, I came to tell you she's locked herself up in her room. And about what happened last night. We're planning what action to take.'

'Okay,' I said and hurried out of the room.

The landlady was resting. She always had a siesta. Perhaps that was why she was still solid, as she herself had said.

It wasn't Thérèse who was at the door.

It was Ndome.

She came in.

I shut the door and locked it. My landlady insisted on the key being turned. It was safer that way, she always said.

'You change them like shirts,' Ndome said in Duala as soon as she entered the room and saw Bibi who was standing by the window. 'And what a large shirt!'

Ndome shook Bibi's hand. There was something imposing about Bibi that made it difficult for one to ignore her.

'*Ndome, ja wase,*' I said.

'I'll sit down,' she said in Duala. 'Don't worry. Let me first admire your woman … *Iyo*, this time it is a baobab.'

'Shut up,' I replied in the same language. 'Can't you shut that useless mouth of yours.'

'You came to study law and not tailoring,' she retorted. 'But since you Cameroonians can do everything, maybe you're also a tailor. Sew up my mouth if you can. I say she's a baobab. Look at her face!'

'Because we're in the West,' I reminded her, 'you seem to have forgotten that a woman can still be beaten.'

'*Na!* That's being very intelligent. *Na!* You can only shout at me. What can you do to a white woman? Ekwe's sits on his head. Touch me! Aren't you ashamed that because of white women you should always be threatening me with a beating? Are you not ashamed? Touch me. I left a policeman round the comer. Try!'

She smiled and I also smiled in spite of myself.

'Anyway,' Ndome said, changing her tone, 'how's the other one?'

'She's well. We're going to get married.'

'What?'

'Ja wa ...'

'Really?'

'Really.'

'You'd marry a white woman?'

'Yes!'

'And this one?'

'She's her friend.'

'Then what is she doing here?'

'Visiting me of course. What else?'

'Nothing. Nothing. What else can she do since she isn't a woman? The things you people do ...'

'Ndome, it is love!'

'You think those girls love you?' she laughed. 'Ekwe will also tell me that his own also loves him. They deceive you people and you accept. They make use of you.'

'My fiancée loves me.'

'Loves you! You're simply deceiving her. As soon as she's pregnant I'll come and ask you about her.'

'It's not they who are deceiving us, it's we who are now deceiving them.'

'You deceive each other.'

'Not me. You'll see.'

'Where?'

'My fiancée? Right to Cameroon!'

'We shall see.'

'Right to Cameroon. *Ná bo-o!*'

'We shall see. Am I old? I still have days left. We shall see …' and, turning to Bibi, she said in French: 'Mademoiselle shake my hand.'

Bibi gave her her hand.

'Are you going already?' I asked in Duala.

'Yes. I am with my fiancé—'

'Where is he?'

'I left the useless thing in the café.'

'And he didn't want to know where you were going?'

'Men want to know everything. I told him I was going to visit a friend of mine, a girl. I couldn't take him with me because the landlady didn't allow male visitors. He's down there, drinking his beer, poor him.'

She smiled.

I went with her to the door and before she went out, she said:

'Leave those white girls alone.'

I didn't smile.

'I heard you,' I said and shut the door and turned the key.

Returning to the room I found Bibi with her handbag in her hand.

'You're also going?'

'Yes.'

'Okay.'

'When do I see you again?'

'Bibi, I don't know. Tomorrow perhaps, but not here. We could have a cup of coffee at the café in which Thérèse introduced me to her mother. You remember it?'

'Why not here?'

'You know why. We've been lucky and things have changed. I don't think it would be advisable for Thérèse to ever meet you here. It would worry her. She might begin to suspect and you know she's delicate. We must spare her unnecessary suffering.'

'But I can no longer remember the café. We went there by car.'

I told her the nearest Métro to the café and explained that the café I meant was the one nearest the Métro. We could meet there the following day at half past four.

Then that door-bell rang again.

'It's Thérèse,' Bibi said.

'I think so too,' I said. 'Look, go into the bathroom. As soon as I lead her in, open the other door, you know, the one that opens into the corridor. Then go to the main door. I'll leave it open. The landlady is resting. There's no risk. Thérèse mustn't see you. I insist.'

Bibi went into the bathroom which had two doors, one that connected with my room and a second door that connected it with the corridor. That was the door Madame Bistrott used.

I went out of the room, walked briskly down the corridor and opened the door. It was Thérèse.

I kissed her on the cheek. She clung to me.

We went to my room and I shut the door. I made her sit on the bed.

'What's wrong?' I asked. 'You look pale.'

'It's nothing,' she breathed.

Naturally she was hesitating to tell me that her father had blown up. She still didn't know about my father's letter.

'Aren't you feeling well?'

'Why?'

'Honestly you look pale.'

She shrugged her shoulders.

I heard the other door of the bathroom whine; then Bibi's footsteps going down the corridor. I am sure Thérèse also heard them. But she must have thought they were the landlady's. However, if she hadn't been preoccupied with her problems and had been a bit suspicious she would have noticed that those footsteps were heavier than Madame Bistrott's. The landlady was a small, emaciated woman and she wore wool-stuffed slippers that absorbed her weight and with the carpet one heard practically no sound when she walked down the corridor. But Bibi was a big woman. She must have been tiptoeing, which explains why the footsteps were a bit light.

'I am in a state of war with my parents,' Thérèse said, staring at the floor, her hands clasped against each other in her lap.

'A state of war?' I asked, calmly.

'Yes,' she nodded.

'Why?'
'My father ...'
'Have you told them?'
'Yes. My father doesn't want ...'

A long silence followed. I wondered whether or not I should tell her about the letter I had received from my father; that this was my last summer in Europe. That she would have to reconsider her earlier engagement to become my wife. The perspective had changed. But how could I tell her that? She was going through a rough time, through anguish and bitterness. The news of my going away by the end of July would add frustration and then despair on her heart, and the way I knew Thérèse I didn't doubt she would be unable to cope at once with acute anguish, acute bitterness, cold frustration and blunt despair. So I decided to keep the news until she was in a better shape.

I put on a record I thought would inspire hope. A violin concerto. But I noticed with disappointment that what I had always taken to be robust now sounded languidly passionate, something so exquisite, those violin strains—something at once beyond hope and despair. The effect on Thérèse was soothing and then exciting. She sighed, then kicked off her shoes from her feet and sank onto the bed, lying on her back, her fingers laced under her head on the pillow.

The room grew intimate. Dusk was falling outside. A mild dusk. The light in the room was developing seams, dark seams; and dressed in this drapery of approaching night Thérèse looked extremely pretty. The rounded lips, the cheeks, the breasts.

'*Doumbe, tu viens?*' she said, inviting me to the bed.

I went and sat on the bed. I unlaced my shoes and took them off; but I didn't take off my trousers and shirt.

I lay down by her side and caressed her cheek and neck.

'Draw the curtains,' she said.

'It doesn't matter,' I said. 'We won't do anything.'

She was pale and weak and oppressed by anguish; and then, with the letter I had received from my father, it didn't seem likely that we would ever become husband and wife. But she had invited me to lie with her because I was her lover who had become her fiancé. To hell with her parents! Perhaps; for we could wait until she was twenty-one. That would be in just over two years' time. But I had under two months left in France. So it was clear that the marriage would never take place, no matter what hopes she was clinging to. To sleep with her now with false hopes in the background seemed to me to be dishonest. So I decided I wouldn't touch her any longer until things had cleared themselves up a little. And then she was weak and pale.

'Doumbe,' she sighed.

'Thérèse …'

Chapter Eight

THE café terrace had the aspect of dawn, because of the lighting. The pavement outside, in the shade of the planetrees, was cool. A few sick leaves having dropped from the branches writhed on the pavement, stirred by the wind.

On the other side of the cross-roads the sun shimmered over the bridge and the Seine. Yellow and red curtains danced against the windows of the tall buildings on the other side of the river. There were curtains of other colours.

Bibi appeared. She was in a navy suit. She pushed the glass door, entered and as she walked to my table she smiled.

She bent down. We kissed. Then she sat down.

'How's everything?' I asked.

'Bad.'

'Thérèse?'

'Yes.'

'What happened?'

'Nothing. She's still not talking to her parents.'

The waiter, a sleek-haired man, came up to us.

Bibi ordered a vanilla ice-cream. I had already had a glass of mineral water.

From our table the waiter went to a man and woman who sat three tables away from ours.

The terrace wasn't crowded because it wasn't sunny. But then I had never seen the café really crowded like the cafés in the Latin Quarters or those in Montparnasse, Montmartre or the Champs Elysées.

Bibi was served her ice-cream. She thanked the waiter and began to eat the ice-cream.

'When did Thérèse get home last night?' I asked after a long silence.

'At dinner-time. We were at table when she came in; but she didn't join us.'

'What did her parents say?'

'They looked at each other, said nothing and went on with the meal; but they didn't seem to have much appetite. I hadn't any myself.'

She took some ice-cream in her tea spoon and held it to me.

'Have a taste,' she said.

'No, thank you,' I said.

'Taste it.'

'No.'

We didn't speak again until she had finished her ice-cream. She carefully wiped her lips with a tiny handkerchief. She sat back, crossed her legs and unbottoned her jacket. Her blouse was white. It was open at the neck and it looked very smart.

'Did she hear me leave yesterday?' Bibi asked.

'No. You said she didn't eat last night?'

'She didn't. She wouldn't join us. She's like that. When she's boycotting her parents she also boycotts meals.'

'And her health suffers.'

'That's what is disturbing about it.'

'And this afternoon? She had lunch?'

'No.'

'But how can she starve herself like that?'

'Perhaps she ate before coming in last night.'

'I don't think so. I wanted to take her out to dinner but she didn't want to. She left me at the entrance of the Métro and said she was going home. She took a taxi and I imagine she went straight home. When did you say she got to the house?'

'Around eight-thirty.'

'She couldn't have stopped on the way. We left my room at eight.'

'Poor girl. Listen, Doumbe, you should have seen her ask me if I thought you loved her!'

'When did she ask you that? Last night?'

'No, this morning. She was the first to get up. I heard a knock on my door and when I opened it it was Thérèse. She came and sat on my bed and then she asked me if I thought you loved her.'

'Why should she have asked that?'

'You know Thérèse is like that. Her main problem is that she imagines people don't love her. Not even her parents.'

'But do they?'

'They love Thérèse very much. It was that love which spoilt her. They've never been able to impose their will on her. In consolation they congratulate themselves on the fact—or fiction—that they brought her up on modern lines, without unnecessary severity, which they claim frustrates children.'

'I thought you said her father was severe …'

'He's noisy, that's all. At the end he bows down to Thérèse. True.'

'They're right.'

'About what?'

'About bringing her up along modern lines as you call it.'

'Right? The result has been catastrophic. It's not only she who is frustrated but they too are frustrated, completely. They fear to incur her enmity and yet it cultivates itself, it grows.'

'I'm very worried about her.'

'We all are. But tell me, Doumbe, why should she have wanted to know from me if you loved her or not? You had a fight yesterday?'

'She wanted us to … you know?'

'Make love?'

'Yes.'

'And you refused?'

'Yes. For certain reasons.'

She smiled and then sighed. She leaned forward and took my hand in hers.

'We're in a mess,' she said.

'How can we get out of it?'

'I know how.'

'How?'

'Promise you won't be offended. You won't be angry.'

'It depends on what you'd say.'

'I think we shouldn't continue to make love. It's unfair. I mean because of Thérèse.'

'Agreed.'

It was clear she hadn't expected that quick and curt reply. She let go my hand and stared at me.

'You love Thérèse,' she mused. 'I can see you do.'

'What about you? You love Laurent.'

'I don't love him.'

'I thought you did. I love Thérèse.'

'I don't believe you.'

'Because you don't want to believe me.'

'Not that.'

'What then?'

'You couldn't love her and then be making love to me.'

'Who told you that? And besides, we won't do it again.'

'Supposing I want it.'

'That's your business. I don't want it. It's over. I'm going.' I took a few francs from my pocket and put them on the table. 'Are you staying? Well, okay …'

I got up. But she held my hand.

'Stay,' she said. 'Please.'

'No. Tell Thérèse that I'll be waiting for her at home. I'll be in all evening.'

I shook off her hand. Two or three people noticed the incident.

I walked out of the café.

When I got to Madame Bistrott's I went into the sitting room and sat down. The landlady liked to talk with me.

'Shall I offer you some coffee?' she asked.

I didn't want coffee. But I knew it would please her to make coffee for me. She was very kind.

'Yes, madame,' I said.

She went to the kitchen and returned after a few minutes with the coffee.

She poured out some for me and held the sugar container sideways. I took two pieces and dropped them into the coffee.

'See if you like it,' she said, going to sit down.

She always said that; and of course I always liked her coffee.

The door-bell rang.

'Let's not answer it,' I said. 'It's a girl. I don't want her. She's going to create problems for me.'

'The young mademoiselle? Thérèse, that is her name?'

'No. Her friend.'

'The tall one?'

'Yes.'

The door-bell rang again.

I sipped the coffee. Madame Bistrott was smiling vaguely. Perhaps she was thinking while not wanting to think of youth!

She had a son, François, who was an engineer in Brest. Madame Bistrott told me that François didn't want to get married. She said it was a matter of principle. He didn't want women. She used to say it was funny, wasn't it, that François didn't want women and yet he was such a decent boy; then, she would add, 'he's fifty you know!'

The door-bell rang again:

Chrong!

Madame Bistrott always said she would have loved to have a grandchild. But François didn't want women. Very funny; but it was a matter of principle. It was a principle of his. 'But, mind you,' she would say, 'I love my son. *Oh si! J'aime mon fils …*'

Only it hurt her that she couldn't have a grandchild because François didn't want women. 'His father …' and I would be in for the usual stuff on Monsieur Bistrott, 'a wonderful man, courageous, talented, hard-working, *un homme quoi!*' and the war which seemed only as an excuse for her to talk about her husband's military medal.

The door-bell:

Chrong!

It had begun to be irritating. Luckily, it didn't ring again just then. We heard—or I heard—footsteps on the bare landing. Then the metallic sound of the door of the lift being banged shut.

'She's gone,' I said.

Madame Bistrott smiled.

I put down my cup.

'Was it good?' she asked.

'Very good. Your coffee is so different from that in the cafés.'

She waved her left hand in the air, meaning: cafés? disgusting!

'They put chicory in it,' she said. 'But I make coffee coffee, genuine coffee.'

'Yes. It was very good.'

She leaned back, as if to relax.

'I am glad you liked it,' she said. 'It always pleases me you know? It pleases me that you liked it …'

I got up.

'*Bon*,' I said. 'I'm going to glance at my table.'

'Going to type?'

'No,' I said.

She smiled and I went out to the corridor, and then I saw a note under the door. I picked it up. The handwriting was Thérèse's. I was disappointed because I had thought it was Bibi who had come to the door.

I unfolded the piece of paper and read: 'Victory!!! My parents are inviting you to dinner tonight. A pity you weren't at home. I wanted to kiss you. But I shall look in again. Thérèse.'

Okay, they had accepted, I thought. But what would they say when they learnt about my impending departure? Will they allow Thérèse to leave them, to go with me to Africa?

I decided to talk to Thérèse about my father's letter that evening. Then I'd mention it to her parents at dinner.

Meanwhile I wouldn't touch Thérèse until I knew how things stood, if in spite of the changes she would still be prepared to marry me. In that case, I hoped, I would drop Bibi and Ndome.

I went into my room and took off my jacket.

I stretched myself on the bed and thought of home. In my imagination I saw the season of planting. My mother and aunts and cousins in the fields. I tried to imagine Thérèse working with them.

I got up and went and sat at the table and wrote a short letter to my father. I said I hoped to be home at the end of July, as he had asked me. I was waiting for the money. All my dreams now were to see those lands developed. My forebears had lived and died on them. That was where I also would live and die. Let others live and work in the cities and run the administration and the industries. But I would work with him on the land.

Had he received my last letter? There was something I wanted to tell him in that letter but which I finally didn't because I wanted to give it more thought; also I wanted to see how things would work themselves out. Well, it was about a wife. I was going to get married to a white woman. No, he shouldn't be worried. She was very nice; she was like one of my cousins, nice, hard-working, respectful. She was like a sister …

I wrote about other things; then I signed the letter, put it in an envelope and took it to the post office which was nearby.

As soon as I returned to the room that door-bell rang.

Thérèse! I thought. At least there was news I could give her. I had just written to my parents about her. It would please her to hear that. Then I would tell her about my father's letter.

I hurried down the corridor and opened the door.

It was Bibi.

'Can I come in?' she asked and glanced at her wrist watch.

'Yes,' I said.

She came in; I closed the door and turned the key.

We went to my room.

'Are you angry with me?' she asked.

'No, why?'

'I thought you were, the way you left me at the café. It was so hard making up my mind whether or not to come.'

'Sit down,' I said. No. I wasn't angry.

'To tell the truth,' I said, I didn't like what you said at the café. The point is that I had made up my mind to stop seeing Thérèse intimately. I was counting on you. And then to hear you say you thought we shouldn't do it again; you can imagine the effect it had on me. No, I'm not angry … What did you tell Thérèse when she asked you if you thought I loved her?'

'I told her that you loved her. That you might pretend you didn't, but that was only a pose. That I had observed you very carefully and I had seen how much you loved her. She looked much better after hearing that. I thought of her throughout the time I was in class. You know she wanted to come with me when I was leaving the house. She said she would wait for me at the cafeteria at the Alliance. But I asked her to stay behind and rest. I left her in my room.'

'She's been here.'

'When?'

'A few moments ago. Her parents have consented. I'll have dinner with you all tonight. And I've just written to my father, telling him about Thérèse.'

'Then why do you say you don't want to make love to her any more?'

'Because we had come to found it on the hopes of our getting married. But somehow that didn't seem likely any longer.'

'But you've just said her parents have consented.'

'Yes. The thing is I'm leaving France at the end of next month. My parents want me back home.'

'Thérèse knows?'

'Not yet.'

'I see.'

'So I don't intend to touch her until I know if her parents will maintain their consent in the present circumstances. And she still has to tell me if she's ready to go to Africa now.'

My eyes met Bibi's. What I had just said must have eased her conscience. Mine was eased.

I took a piece of paper and wrote: 'Saw your note. But obliged to absent myself until seventy-thirty. Doumbe.'

I took it to the main door which I opened; and, standing on the landing, I pinned the note on the door so that Thérèse would see it as soon as she came out of the lift.

I returned to the room and drew the curtains, throwing the room into half darkness.

'I haven't much time,' Bibi said, unbuttoning her jacket.

Bibi and I decided we wouldn't see each other in my room any more. I would write to her through the *poste restante* and tell her where and when we could meet. We said that perhaps hotels would do. It would be amusing arriving there like tourists. We didn't want to take any chances with Thérèse. If I wrote Bibi through Monsieur Vaele's address, the letter—one never knew—might fall into Thérèse's hands. We wanted to avoid that possibility.

I walked with Bibi to the door. I opened it and she left.

Apparently Thérèse had come back while Bibi and I had been in the room, for the note had been removed from the door.

I returned to my room.

I had a bath and dressed.

Thérèse arrived at half past seven, looking tired but happy.

We went out almost immediately.

As we went to the Métro, I said:

'Thérèse, I don't know how you'll take it—'

'What?'

'My father has recalled me.'

'Are you joking?'

'No. He wrote last week.'

'Is it because of me?'

'No. I've just written to them about you.'

'Yes?'

'Yes. This afternoon.'

'But is it true that he wants you to return home?'

'Yes.'

'And will you go?'

'Yes. End of July, with you.'

'But my parents?'

'You first say yes. We'll see about your parents later. Eh, Thérèse?'

'What?'

'Would you go with me?'

She was silent for a few seconds; then she said:

'Doumbe, you know?'

'No.'

'I am afraid.'

'Afraid of what? Of Africa?'

'No, Doumbe. Of my parents. They've just accepted that we can marry. I don't know how they'd react to our going away. But I'd love to go away, you know. I'd love to live another life …'

She took my hand.

It was Madame Vaele who opened the door for us. She looked pale and her voice was thin, thinner than it had been that day at the café.

'Come in,' she said. She shook my hand; then, turning

to her daughter, she said: 'Thérèse, you're all charming and radiant—'

'It's not true,' Thérèse spat haughtily.

Her mother smiled; then she said:

'This way.'

We walked down a long red-carpeted corridor.

'This way,' Madame Vaele said again.

We entered the sitting-room. It was a large, lavishly furnished apartment, one of the many that the more or less wealthy classes keep for themselves in Paris. There was a piano, glistening symbol of Western bourgeois culture. The furniture was antique. I have never been particularly interested in old European furniture. I know practically nothing about it; so it would be very difficult to describe the sitting-room in detail.

The upholstery was rich and grimly showy. Two paintings of landscapes hung on the walls. They were huge paintings. They looked to me like shadows in pine woods with a sad, cloudy sky brooding in perspective. I am not sure by whom the paintings were. I didn't get near enough to them for me to read the signatures and I'm not good at detecting the styles of the various masters. I am convinced those paintings were masterpieces by the mere fact that they were in Monsieur Vaele's sitting-room. With a firm in the Ivory Coast and an office in Paris and more funds possibly invested elsewhere, Monsieur Vaele was a rich man. He could afford to buy masterpieces.

'Jacques,' Thérèse's mother called her husband.

'*Oui, Marthe,*' a man's voice—Thérèse's father's voice—replied from an adjoining room.

'Our guest has arrived.'

Monsieur Vaele, an emaciated, bald-headed man of average height, emerged. His forehead shiny, he was in a grey three- piece suit, looking like a Quai d'Orsay diplomat.

In spite of his firm handshake, I was sure he wasn't pleased to see me. He hadn't brought up his daughter for a foreigner. That was a reality. He had brought her up for France, and only a French boy would have been really welcome to him. Or if not a Frenchman, someone from Europe. Not that someone told me all that. I felt it. He didn't like me. But I imagine when my mother was bringing me up and she thought of the woman I'd marry, the idea didn't occur to her that I'd decide to marry a white woman. She must have imagined a Mongo or a Duala girl becoming my wife; or at least a girl from some corner or other of Cameroon. But a white woman! No, that wouldn't have occurred to her. It was in the same way that I imagined Thérèse's parents didn't dream of an African becoming their son-in-law.

'I am very glad to make your acquaintance,' Monsieur Vaele nevertheless said. 'How do you do?'

In French, unlike in English, one doesn't just repeat the same question, so I said:

'Very well, *merci!*'

Thérèse hadn't even been able to introduce her father. He had bounced forward, oblivious of protocol unlike his compatriots at the Quai. He had bounced forward, towards me, his hand out, and then said how glad he was and all that. I thought he did it deliberately. He didn't want Thérèse to introduce him. He wanted to deal her that affront. His reasons were obvious. But then I was only speculating. That might not have been his intention. But I noticed the man's forwardness made Thérèse nervous. She fingered one of the buttons of her jacket, but almost immediately removed her hand from it and looked at her shoes.

Her father, having shaken my hand, asked me to sit down.

'I'm coming,' Thérèse said to us and hurried out of the room, followed by her mother.

'*Alors*,' Monsieur Vaele said, dipping his hand into his pocket and leaning back in his chair. 'How do you like our country?'

I said one couldn't complain any more as the cold was over. With the sun and the sky so blue, it was like Africa in the dry season. 'It's agreeable,' I concluded.

'Umm,' he said, sitting up and opening his cigarette case. He held it to me.

'I don't smoke, thanks,' I said.

'Never?'

'Never.'

'That's very good.'

He lit one and while he smoked, we talked.

'Talking about Africa,' he said, 'I'm going there tomorrow, to the Ivory Coast.'

'Yes?'

'Yes,' he nodded, blowing out the smoke, his chin almost resting on his tie.

He leaned backwards, closed his eyes, smoking, his forehead wrinkled. I thought he was thinking of something or was refusing to think of something.

'For how long?' I asked.

'Three days,' he said opening his eyes and crossing his legs. 'Three days.'

'Only?'

He nodded deeply, pouting, giving himself a decisive and authoritative air. 'To have a look round, put one or two things in order and then back to Paris,' he said and replaced his cigarette between his lips.

I noticed his eyes were tragically mocking, as if he were thinking: I'll put you in your place! He had a large nose. He had a way of looking at me as if he wasn't seeing me clearly, or perhaps it was only the cigarette smoke that was hampering his view.

There was something about Mr. Vaele's face that left the impression of embarrassment, a subtle suffering. But if he had problems, he seemed to be bearing them as a man should, calmly, tactfully, lucidly; and that was admirable.

It's with an effort that I try to reach an objective appraisal of his personality for I was prejudiced against him following the amount of information I already had about him from Bibi, and even from Thérèse. I sympathized with him. The world wasn't an easy place and nature didn't seem to be inclined to make things easy for people. I sensed Monsieur Vaele's suffering and I became indulgent. He could have been my father's friend. But he looked younger. Monsieur Vaele must have been fifty. Thérèse had never told me her father's age; because I never asked it. She said her mother was forty-five.

'Is it a beautiful country, the Ivory Coast?' I asked. 'I've never been there.'

'Not bad as a country,' he said, freely. 'Abidjan is a beautiful city. The people are nice, hospitable. And they're not as xenophobic as certain African countries are regrettably becoming.'

'Not many years ago, they expelled Dahomeans. There was plenty of violence at the time.'

'Yes, you're right. It's true. But all that has past. It's over. And you in Cameroon?'

'It's five years since I've not been home, so I don't know. Africa changes rapidly.'

'But it seemed to me I heard you've been only two years in France?'

'That's right. Before coming to France I was in Nigeria.'

'Great country.'

'Have you been there?'

'Not yet. But I suppose I'll go there one day. I'd very much like to tour the whole of Africa—'

'It's wonderful, to be able to travel—'

'I adore travelling. It refreshes the mind; one relaxes,

one breathes … What other countries of Europe have you visited?'

'None.'

'Of course in two years one can't do much; and you've had your studies—'

'The thing is I won't be able to visit them any longer. Even my studies, I'd have to abandon them.'

'How's that? I don't understand.'

'My father wants me back—'

'When?'

'End of July.'

Very strangely, his face relaxed. He smoked in silence for a minute or two before taking his cigarette between his fingers; and, leaning to his right, his arm on the arm of the chair, he asked:

'Thérèse knows?'

'Yes,' I replied.

Now he knotted his lips and nodded, his forehead wrinkling.

'Umm,' he breathed. 'That's new.'

I thought I should explain things more pointedly.

'My father has attained a certain age,' I said. 'It's normal that he should want me to be near him.'

Monsieur Vaele smiled. 'Monsieur,' he said, 'all parents are the same. All parents want their children to be near them. What would you say if I told you that I want Thérèse, for example, to be near me? I too have attained a certain age.'

'That's a delicate question, Monsieur Vaele.'

'It's not only delicate. It's also difficult to answer because if your father has the right to ask you to return to Africa and you're obeying, I think as a father I too have the same right over Thérèse.'

'It's not the same thing, monsieur.'

He smiled again, tucked the cigarette between his lips and smoked for a few seconds. Then he said:

'Don't be worried. I only wanted you to see the situation in which you have thrown us. It's not easy.'

'I know, monsieur—'

'So think it over …'

'I know it's difficult for you. But it isn't any easier for me either. I would have loved to stay and complete my studies.'

'Then stay.'

'I can't.'

'With your level of studies can you find suitable work, in the administration for example?'

'I'm not going into the administration. I'm going to work with my parents on the land. I am going to the village.'

'Yes?'

'You shouldn't feel worried, Monsieur Vaele. Thérèse might find it a bit difficult to get accustomed to the climate, but I think with time she should be able to stand it.'

'I don't know about that. Look at my wife. The doctors advise her never to set foot in the tropics … *Non*,

I would have preferred both of you to remain in Europe. Your future would be more assured, more certain; but in Africa?' He raised his eyebrows. 'With the exception of certain countries, the situation in Africa isn't encouraging.'

'It will change.'

He closed his eyes. When he opened them, he said:

'Give me your address. I'll drop you a word as soon as I return from Abidjan.'

I gave him the address. He wrote it in his pocket book. I had to spell out my name, several times, for him. Not several times. But I did some repetition. He pocketed the book.

Thérèse came in.

'What are you two saying?' she asked, with a frown, as if she had a headache.

'We're conversing, the two of us,' Monsieur Vaele said. 'Thérèse, won't Bibi come and be introduced to—'

'Doumbe,' Thérèse said.

'Doumbe,' her father repeated, glancing at me.

'Yes,' I said, with a smile.

'It's a typically Bantu name.'

'My tribe is Bantu—at least that's what the books say.'

We laughed. Thérèse didn't laugh very much. But she smiled. 'Bibi?' Monsieur Vaele said to Thérèse. 'Go and bring her—' 'Directly,' the girl said.

'Or maybe they know each other already?'

Now Thérèse laughed, very frankly, but innocently too. 'I think so,' she said.

But if he had guessed rightly about Bibi he didn't suspect I had already been introduced to his wife in town. And Madame Vaele, apparently to amuse herself, said, when we were at table:

'You still have your parents?'

Thérèse moved in her chair. Her eyes didn't leave the plate before her. Bibi was calm, concentrating on the meal. Only Monsieur Vaele seemed to take an innocent interest in the question his wife had asked, and he said:

'Yes, at least his father. He's asking him to return to Africa, at the end of July … That's right, eh? The end of July?'

'Yes,' I said.

Madame Vaele looked at her daughter.

'She knows,' her husband said hurriedly, wiping his mouth with his napkin. 'She knows …'

Chapter Nine

Thérèse's father wrote to me towards the end of June. He asked me if I could have dinner with him in a restaurant on the Right Bank. He said I needn't reply if I could be there. He mentioned all the particulars: the name of the restaurant, the street, the number of the street, the nearest Métro. The day was a Wednesday. The time: eight o'clock. He asked me to be discreet. He wanted us to have a little chat and he thought it would be unwise to let Thérèse know about it. He hoped I understood.

I didn't reply and on the given Wednesday I went to the restaurant, exactly at eight. I found him already there. He hadn't the air of a prospective father-in-law.

He talked about Abidjan. We began to eat. Green salad, a leaf each, which carried a boiled egg with mayonnaise. The waitress was a thickly made-up middle-aged woman.

By the time we had finished with the salad and eggs, Monsieur Vaele had exhausted such information as he could give me about his three-day visit to the Ivory Coast.

The waitress cleared our plates. Monsieur Vaele poured himself a glass of red wine and drank half of it.

We waited in silence for the second course.

Monsieur Vaele drank from his glass again and wiped his mouth with his napkin. He put it down, between him and the table.

The waitress arrived with steak and frites.

We began to eat.

Monsieur Vaele emptied his glass of wine and refilled it. Then he said:

'It's very delicate, what I want us to discuss.'

He lowered his eyes. We continued with the meal in silence until I asked, calmly:

'I suppose you want to talk about Thérèse?'

He looked up from his plate.

'Yes,' he said. 'It's about Thérèse. I prefer to be frank. That girl is a child. We suffer, my wife and I. And it's not easy. Thérèse is our only child you know.'

'I know, Monsieur Vaele.'

He put half of his energy into cutting the steak, while with the other half he asked:

'Is everything calm in Cameroon?'

'What do you mean?'

'I mean calm—'

'There was a revolution going on, but it's hard to tell what's happening now.'

'I don't know what will happen,' he said, and ate the tiny piece of steak he had cut.

I let him finish chewing it while I was chewing what I had in my mouth.

'You mean what will happen to Thérèse?' I asked.

'No,' Monsieur Vaele asserted. 'It's about you that I am worried. Or rather I am worried about both of you. White people are no longer popular in Africa.'

'They will be when we also become popular in Europe and America.'

He drank half his glass of wine and putting down the glass he again applied his fork and knife on the steak. It wasn't easy to cut.

A long silence followed during which we finished the steak and frites. I mean finished with it; because although I emptied my plate, Monsieur Vaele didn't eat as much as half his steak and he left some frites on his plate. He didn't seem to have much appetite. The other day at his place he had eaten better; and he had been livelier in spite of everything. He had even been a bit talkative, a shade flippant. But today he was moody; he looked extremely tired. The wine, however, was improving his spirits.

The waitress came and removed our plates. Monsieur Vaele fingered the knot of his tie. His hand dropped to his belly and took hold of his napkin. He wiped his mouth again. He shoved the napkin back between the table and him and took the glass of wine and emptied it. Putting it down, he refilled the glass. He was beginning to look a bit pleased with himself.

'Are you finding it difficult to tell me that you are opposed to my marrying Thérèse?' I asked.

'Difficult?' he asked, sitting back to take his napkin in his hands. 'I don't think that's the word.'

He wiped his mouth with the napkin and put it down, on the table this time.

The waitress served us with cheese.

'Thanks,' I said to her.

'Thanks,' Monsieur Vaele said, taking the napkin from the table to return it between his belly and the edge of the table.

I don't think he was very nervous. But one thing was certain: he was trying to remain calm and my secret attitude was sympathetic. I knew it was I who had put him in this situation. It wasn't easy at all.

'Difficult!' he mused, pouting and nodding slightly, his forehead wrinkling.

He put some cheese on a piece of bread, and glanced at me.

'That's the impression I have,' I said.

He ate the piece of bread and cheese. His face had become red.

'I don't know if that's the way to put it,' he said. 'But perhaps you're right. It's not always easy not to be able to demonstrate one's goodwill. It's not always easy …'

We went on with the cheese, in silence.

I finished mine. He also finished his; but that was because with cheese you helped yourself. So you cut just the quantity you thought you could finish. It was good Normandy cheese; it stank. But the stink didn't matter. In fact some people liked it the more it stank.

Monsieur Vaele wiped his mouth. I wiped mine. The

waitress cleared our plates. Monsieur Vaele emptied his third glass of wine. Before the waitress carried our plates away she asked us what we would have for dessert.

'An apple,' I said.

Monsieur Vaele:

'A banana.'

'*Très bien,*' the waitress said and hurried away with our plates and the tray of cheese.

Thérèse's father leaned back in his chair and put his hand in the pocket of his jacket. It came out with a handkerchief with which he mopped his brow.

He replaced his handkerchief in his pocket and passing his left hand over his bald head, he said:

'You are young, monsieur. A white woman would be very embarrassing for you in Africa. Don't you think?'

'No,' I said, shaking my head. 'I wouldn't be the first African to take a white woman to Africa. In fact there are many there, unmarried, who work in government offices, in the firms, to earn their living. Naturally there'd be less and less, especially in the administration. But the fact remains that there'll always be white women in Africa.'

'I know, but—'

The waitress, putting a plate on which there was a knife and a banana before Monsieur Vaele, said:

'*Voilà une banane …*'

'Thanks,' Monsieur Vaele said, gloomily.

Then putting before me a plate on which was an apple and a knife, she said, elegantly:

'*... et une pomme.*'

'Thanks,' I said.

'Would you want some coffee afterwards?' she asked, staring into Monsieur Vaele's eyes in a way that suggested 'dear monsieur we could have some fun if you're serious.'

'Yes,' Thérèse's father said. 'For me.'

'*Et monsieur?*' asked the waitress, smiling stiffly. But her eyes were true. They were alert. They seemed highly sensitive to charm. But neither Thérèse's father nor I could have been charming that evening. Not because we had worries. No. It was simply that we couldn't flirt in each other's presence. And to many French women a charming man was precisely the man who was ready to flirt in a light-hearted, entertaining sort of way with enough seriousness nevertheless to convince a woman that if she showed that she was interested he would act. To be the exact opposite of that was to be *peu intéressant*. And a woman could despise a man who wasn't interesting. The waitress was smiling.

I shook my head, pouting.

'No?' she asked.

I nodded.

She went to fetch Monsieur Vaele's coffee.

Thérèse's father offered me a cigarette.

I reminded him that I didn't smoke.

'I thought you smoked at the house the other day,' he said with the air of someone who is trying to recall something connected with the conversation in hand.

'No,' I said. 'Never.'

'Ah?' he said, unwrinkling his forehead as he lit his cigarette.

He smoked for about a minute. The restaurant wasn't crowded. There were a number of couples, eating. Others had finished eating. They talked, in almost inaudible voices. Some had their elbows on the table; others, the more self-conscious ones, hid their arms between the tables and their bellies. They leaned forward, as if obliged to show politeness and deference towards their partners. Some talked over coffee. Others talked over table cloths that carried nothing besides ashtrays. A man ate by himself a few tables away from ours. It was rare to see a woman eating all alone in those plush restaurants.

Monsieur Vaele's coffee arrived. He thanked the waitress and asked her for the bill. She said it would be ready in a minute.

'You know,' I said. 'If you don't want me to marry Thérèse you must say so. I'd rather know where I stand than waste my time for nothing. If you don't want it, say so. I wouldn't marry a woman without her parents' consent, not even if she were of age. Marriage is not between two persons. It is between two families. That is how it is in Africa. Marriage brings two families together, not just two persons.'

'It's a very good way of looking at it. Do your parents know about Thérèse?'

'I suppose they do by now.'

'Why, because you've just written to them?'

'Yes, about a fortnight ago.'

'And they haven't replied?'

'That's right.'

'And you think they'd agree?'

'I can't see them refusing. They'd understand. Things have changed in Africa.'

'Indeed; but certain things are very difficult to change.'

'I don't think so. It's impressive the way Africa is losing many of its old prejudices.'

'It's evolution—'

'Granted. But look at Europe. Look at America. You don't seem to be losing your prejudices. One would say you have ceased to evolve.'

He definitely didn't like that for he didn't say anything for nearly a minute. He smoked and sipped his coffee. No, for more than a minute.

Then the waitress returned with the bill. It was on a plate. She returned to the kitchen or wherever it was from which she brought the plates.

Monsieur Vaele crushed the butt of his cigarette in the ashtray.

He said, leaning forward, his hands clasped on the table:

'Let's reason together. You said you wouldn't marry my daughter if I were against it, not even if she were of age?'

'Yes.'

'Well, I don't want her to go away. I am very much attached to Thérèse. If I had another child, perhaps. But I haven't, and Africa is too far away. I hope you understand how I feel about it?'

'About Africa?'

'No. About Thérèse.'

'I see …'

'I know you are disappointed; and I also know it's only you who can help me now.'

'Help you, how?'

'Thérèse mustn't know of my decision. If she does she'd be furious with me. And her anger can be terrible.'

'You really mean you're against our getting married?'

'I am obliged to be—'

'And Thérèse shouldn't know?'

'It would be preferable if she didn't …'

'And how am I to settle it with her?'

He pursed his lips; his forehead wrinkled thoughtfully. He craned his neck, his chin out; then his forehead became smooth and shiny again. He moved in his chair, glanced rapidly at his clasped hands and then, looking at me, he said:

'If you told her you couldn't marry her any longer, the effect would be the same as her learning of my decision. So I can't advise you to tell her that what you planned has become impossible.'

'So what should I say to her?'

'I'd rather prefer your waiting until a week or so before your departure.'

'And tell her what?'

'I know it isn't easy for you. I know you love her and I am grateful to you for it …'

'But what will I tell Thérèse?'

'That you're going ahead. That she can join you after you've made preparations for her arrival. We shall advise her to be patient.'

'Won't it be said tomorrow that it was I who abandoned her?'

'Why?'

'Because people say black men make use of white women and then leave them with children and without means …'

He certainly didn't like the way I put it. *Use!* It was rather cruel of me to have employed such a word about women in a conversation with a man whose daughter was going through the same thing; or, to put it more bluntly, through whose daughter the same thing was going. Not that I said it intentionally. No. It is now that I am writing about it that it all sounds cruel. But I remember he didn't like it all. At least his face showed that he didn't like the way I put it. He didn't appreciate the way I put it. But then he was a father and fathers simply don't appreciate such manners.

'Is she expecting a child?' he asked, painfully, uneasily.

'No,' I said, pleased that I could say no. For otherwise, what anguish!

'So there are no problems,' he sighed without hiding his great relief.

'But supposing she asks that we get married before I leave?'

'We could always make it seem possible. June will soon

end. Let her know of your plans for going away without her only at the last minute. Not exactly at the last minute. But let's say, ten days or a week before your departure, when there would no longer be time to arrange the legal formalities. That's all we can do. And, monsieur, I must say how very grateful I am to you for having been so understanding. I hope you understand that I'm not against you personally. Never! Only my situation is so difficult that common sense counsels the solution I have just suggested.'

Chapter Ten

THÉRÈSE continued to hope, and by the end of June her very life seemed inseperable from her hope of going to Africa, as my wife. She was naturally happy not knowing what her father and I had decided. Somehow I felt I had to keep my word to her father; so I didn't whisper a thing to Thérèse, knowing how violent and self-destructive her reaction was likely to be.

I couldn't say I wouldn't make love to her any more. That would have made her suspect immediately that something had happened or was about to happen. It would have interfered with her happiness; and for a girl who thought of herself as being ugly, a girl who was subject to frequent moments of depression, to see her gay, happy, was something beautiful; and I wanted to help her remain that way. That was why I resumed making love to her after nearly a fortnight's abstinence. No. A fortnight? I'm not sure. But what I remember was that we resumed active intimacy a few days after that dinner at their place; and by the time I received her father's invitation to the dinner during which it had been decided that I couldn't marry Thérèse, we had become so addicted to our desires that we did things lavishly, exaggeratedly even. Thérèse felt free with me, more than she had felt in the past because not only her mother, but her father also knew about us. And I had been invited to their place and had had dinner with them, not as a friend of the family, but as the man who had proposed to her, the man she had accepted and whom she had forced her parents to accept.

I also felt freer; for I had told them about my father and the land and the life Thérèse and I would lead in Africa. And then with no examinations to sit, I didn't think of my law books any more. I read a novel from time to time. And I wrote.

Thérèse too was free from academic preoccupations for she was going to Africa at the end of July! To hell with Geography and the Sorbonne.

I remember how a couple of days following the dinner with her father in the Right Bank restaurant Thérèse arrived at my place and slumped on the bed, kicking off her shoes.

'It's incredible how peaceful I feel,' she said.

I kissed her and again kissed her. It was so agreeable kissing her. I had hated to kiss, but with Thérèse I came to realize how nice it could be; then I remembered that I had run out of contraceptives. I told her. She said it wouldn't disturb anybody. But why, I said, we had to be careful. She said just as I wanted. But she thought I had once said I wanted a child. I said that was true but that I had no intention of having my child conceived under foreign skies. We'd have to wait until we got home. She kissed me and I left the bed, put on my shoes, dressed and went to a pharmacy that was two blocks away.

I gave the young lady the bit of paper with the trade mark that showed I was already a customer. The young lady glanced at it and gave it back to me. She was in overalls. She went to one end of the counter, bent down and when she straightened up again, she asked me if I wanted a packet of six or of twelve. I said twelve. She bent down again and straightened up. She had it in her hand. She gave it to me and I paid. As I moved to go she smiled at me from the corner of her eye. She was very nice. She always smiled whenever I bought them; and she always smiled from the corner of her eye. She hadn't a ring on her finger and perhaps she too was a customer of her boy friend. Yes. So she understood and I think she was pleased because I was being reasonable.

June ended and July, sunny and hot, proved to be a very nervous month indeed, a month in a hurry. I saw Laurent twice, first on the Boulevard Saint Michel and then in the University Restaurant. We didn't talk to each other. He didn't see me; or he pretended he didn't see me.

Meanwhile Bibi was showing signs of falling in love; or that was what I thought out of vanity. She was serene; talked less, and never about Laurent.

At the beginning of the second week in July I decided to do away with all precautions with Thérèse. I took the decision out of love. I had thought over the situation. There was something true and human about Thérèse that deepened my feelings for her; sometimes I thought if I didn't marry her, I'd never marry another woman. Countries and distances and oceans and seas separated my people from hers and the mountains and deserts were a fact, an undeniable reality; but the basic reality was love, and that was what now held us together in spite of her father. But I wasn't angry with Monsieur Vaele. I knew he too acted out of love for Thérèse. Only his was a different kind of love. I loved his daughter. I was sure of that; and it was with a deep uneasiness that I discovered that Bibi was also present in my heart whenever I thought of Thérèse. Perhaps if Thérèse officially became my wife, I'd change; perhaps I'd be faithful to her, for the truth was that I wished I could be faithful to her. Sometimes I wished I hadn't gone so far with Bibi. But I vowed I'd discipline myself when Thérèse became my wife. I was bent on making it possible. That was why I decided to do away with all precautions. I thought that if Thérèse became pregnant it might force her father's hand.

Thérèse was so happy that I decided to be nakedly natural with her. But the following day I regretted what I had done. I couldn't gamble with her life. And three days after that afternoon of complete nakedness I switched back to limited intimacy and Thérèse simply couldn't understand why. She said so. Why? *Eh, pourquoi?* I said I thought we were taking an unwise risk. We had all our tomorrows. There was no worry. I kissed her and that was that.

Meanwhile she was buying books on Africa: sociology, ethnography, history, even politics. She said she wanted a whole library. I told her that that would be too much of a load. She said the books would follow us by sea. By sea of course, because we were to leave by air! I told her there would be other things to do besides reading. She said it didn't matter. After the day's work what else would be as interesting as reading in bed, waiting for sleep in the yellow light of a hurricane lamp? she asked. Her memory and her imagination had become so alive, so active. What I used to talk to her about now returned to my ears in a slightly altered form, from her own lips. She talked in anticipation of the Mungo River, the great birds on its banks. The moon on a real forest. A meek moon. And of my aunts and cousins and little sisters. It would be wonderful, she said, learning to make the river sound like drums. She too would cry messages after planes and egrets, messages to 'this France of which I have had enough.' And she added: 'You can't imagine how glad I am to be able to go away. I think I'm too universal to be tied down to Europe. I feel something in me, something that grows while the days shorten and our departure approaches. To exile myself in the future, Doumbe, to hope and be free, to love and perhaps be loved.'

'What I find amusing,' I had said in reply, 'is that I am taking you as a hostage. When the interventionists begin to bomb our part of Africa you will die, like me, in the struggle. How would you like that?'

'It doesn't frighten me any longer,' she said. 'I even feel that is the way I shall end.'

'And you don't care?'

'I don't. It would be the best way to die, because it was foreseen and chosen. I prefer to choose the way I'll die. Many people would also like to be able to choose. But they can't. What they do is to choose the manner in which their remains will be disposed of. But I prefer to choose how I'll die. So you see? Bombs! I have chosen Africa, because I've chosen you. But my corpse would be miserable if you abandoned it. Eh, Doumbe, would you abandon it?'

'A corpse poses no problems. It is you, dear Thérèse, that I care for. I care for you, the living Thérèse—'

'I want to believe you, Doumbe. But I have doubts.'

'You are afraid.'

'No. I'm no longer afraid. Fear is a weakness, it is a kind of blindness. But doubt is lucid. It is an enlarged vision. Fear? No; that's over. I'd go with you anywhere, even if it were to die; but on condition that you want me. If you do, what is fear?'

'You sound heroic.'

'Does it displease you?'

'No.'

'I'm becoming myself. My mother says she can't understand me any longer—as if she had ever understood me.'

'I'm very glad.'

'What do you mean by that?'

'What?'

'That you are glad. Is it irony or what?'

'Not at all. You think it was enchanting to see you morose, depressed, glum, as you had the habit of being? I told you you would change and you are changing every day. It's reassuring.'

And today, a Wednesday, we were in the Luxembourg Gardens. I thought of Bibi. We didn't see each other very frequently. And the few times we met it was in hotels. But tomorrow, Thursday, which was the day she had her afternoon off, we were due to meet in a hotel in the Rue Cler. After thinking of Bibi I thought of Thérèse. Why had I taken that risk with her? If she became pregnant? Would it help? Or would it inflame her father the more? If I was going away, I had to do so without leaving children behind; I had to go away without leaving behind an image of mine, something of myself growing away from me.

Thérèse leaned against the back of the wooden bench on which we were sitting.

Behind the trees of the gardens and the roofs of the buildings beyond them, the west was full of colours. But they gradually paled for the sun was no longer visible. The night was already on the horizon.

'You're suddenly so silent,' Thérèse said. 'What are you thinking about?'

'Nothing.'

'Nothing!'

I nodded.

'Nothing, absolutely nothing,' I said.

'It's not true,' she said and turned to face me. She looked into my eyes. 'See, I can read many things.'

'Yes?'

'Yes.'

I got up. She also got up. And as we walked towards the exit, I said:

'I can't see you tomorrow—'

'Why?' she asked.

'I want to go to the embassy. It's time we began the formalities of the marriage. You know we have practically no time left. Two weeks, that's nothing. It's ridiculous that up to now we've done nothing.'

'It's true—'

'But I can always write to my father and say I can't come until, say, the middle of August—'

'I think that's what we shall have to do … So you're going to the embassy tomorrow?'

'Yes. I want to discuss one or two things with the Consul General.'

'I'll come with you.'

'No.'

'But why?'

'You mustn't follow me all over the place. I'm sorry but it's not like that in Africa. My mother doesn't follow my father wherever he goes.'

'*Bon d'accord.* You go to the embassy in the morning. And in the afternoon? Can't we meet in the afternoon?'

'I'll have other things to do.'

Immediately she looked sad.

'I don't understand,' she said.

I put my arm round her shoulders and kissed her. It reassured her.

'I'll see you on Friday,' I said.

We took the train at Luxembourg Station, changed at Denfert and got on to the Etoile line.

At La Motte-Picquet I kissed Thérèse on the lips, briefly, and whispered that I'd wait for her at home on Friday, at five, and jumped out of the train.

'Greet Bibi for me,' I cried, just as the door clanged shut. Thérèse nodded. The train pulled out of the station. She looked back and waved.

Chapter Eleven

THE hotel in the Rue Cler smelt of arrivals and hopes and passions and departures and more arrivals and more departures. The in-coming odour of sweat and the out-going scent of perfume.

The receptionist, slender, flame-lipped, with the black night thickly fringing her eyes, checked my reservation.

'A double-room,' she said, her finger going down her register.

'A double-room.'

'I have already paid—'

'To me?'

'No. There was another woman—'

'*En effet*. Monsieur Doumbe. Is that right?'

'That's right.'

'Yes, everything is in order …'

She gave me a form to fill in. Name and date and place of birth and things like that. Number of passport. Date of first entry in France.

As I was filling the form a Japanese with two cameras strapped about him walked to the desk and began to talk to the receptionist. The Japanese wasn't very tall. He was dressed as an American. One minute later his wife joined him. She wasn't dressed as an American woman. She was dressed as a Japanese woman and she looked shy. It was strange how Oriental women rarely looked one in the face. I can't remember any—no, one did—who looked me boldly in the face. The wife of the Japanese didn't look at me at all. But I guess it's that vanity that some men have. Why should she have looked at me, any way? She didn't. But women did; and one gets into the habit of meeting bold eyes, women's eyes, looking at one no matter how discreetly.

The wife of the Japanese didn't look at me at all. She held her eyes on the flame-lipped receptionist who looked very elegant and relaxed and without worries, and who looked as though she would do that job all her life and live all her life in Paris.

The Japanese was asking her about the night places. No. I am not sure what he was asking her. It's quite some time ago, all that, and one forgets certain things; and besides, I don't think I paid enough attention; I had that form to fill in. But I remember thinking: it's curious that Oriental women don't look at men in the face; perhaps they only look at their men. But it must be different in the Orient. The Japanese was a very small man. He looked as light and as practical as a transistor set. The conversation with the receptionist ended with profuse thanks from the Japanese. He went and joined his shy wife and began to say something to her.

I gave the form I had filled in to the receptionist.

'*Très bien,*' she said with a pompous air. She gave me my key.

Two girls brushed passed me. One of them held out her hand to the receptionist who gave her a key.

'We are two,' I said. 'The second person would be arriving around four-thirty. Kindly send her up please.'

'*Entendu,*' she said. 'But she will have to register.'

'Of course,' I said and smiled.

The two girls were of Thérèse's height, that is my height, which means they weren't very tall. They wore scarfs on their heads, the two girls; scarfs knotted under their chins. They had slim legs and they wore canvas shoes. They were now on the staircase. They climbed slowly and they talked as they climbed.

The girls stopped on the third floor and I continued to the fourth.

I opened the door of my room. It was a charming room, agreeable. A fine bed. A modern wardrobe not like that huge old thing with its misty mirror at Madame Bistrott's. Here the wardrobe was modern and the mirror was clean. The wash-stand was screened. The window overlooked a deep courtyard. Pigeons flew about. Some dropped like leaves towards the courtyard below, and they cooed. To see pigeons dropping like that then flying up again, their lives apparently circumscribed by the paved courtyard below and the walls of the buildings, is a depressing sight. To live under the eaves and to fly up and down. For how long? If I could care about pigeons one would understand why sometimes thinking of Thérèse became a melancholy experience. And then although we had plenty of fun it shouldn't be assumed that I took her to bed very often; nor that I took women to bed very often. With Bibi, because of the clandestine nature of our affair, things happened only occasionally. And Ndome, the African girl, had her fiancé. We saw each other about once a fortnight. It was a pity that Thérèse's father had refused to let the girl build her life with mine. I know I wouldn't have been faithful to her, even after marriage; but I would have made the effort to be faithful.

I yawned and moved away from the window as if with the thought: let the skies take care of the pigeons; sleep must now take care of my eyes. I yawned again.

It was two in the afternoon. I hoped Thérèse hadn't conceived. But that weekend was the time when she would normally be in a position to know. I was worried. Luckily I was feeling sleepy.

I took off my jacket, and put it away in the wardrobe. Then my tie, shirt, shoes and finally my trousers. I put the tie and the shirt and the trousers, like the jacket, in the wardrobe.

From the travelling bag I had brought with me I took out a pair of pyjamas which I put on and got under the bed-clothes.

I was awakened by a knock on the door.

I pushed away the bed-clothes and strode sleepily to the

door and opened it. I returned to the bed; determined to go back to sleep.

A few minutes later Bibi was in the bed; but my back was turned towards her.

Sleep returned to my eyes …

When later I woke up, Bibi was fast asleep. I tried to go back to sleep but I couldn't. I felt gay and strong. Not gay; but I felt I was in wonderful shape, refreshed, all worries gone. I had been asleep for nearly four hours! Does plenty of good, sleep. I forgot about Thérèse; forgot about the fact that my father had still not replied to my letter. But perhaps it didn't matter any longer. Not that I thought that while I was feeling so good, so happy because of the siesta. I had thought about that before. Bibi. I put my palm on her forehead, smoothed her hair backwards. I laid my lips on her cheek, my hand on one of her breasts.

Her bosom rose as she breathed in. Her bosom fell with her breathing out.

She opened her eyes, large eyes. She turned and lay on her side and stretched an arm which she put on my side, her hand on my back, just below the scruff of my neck.

Was it right—what we were doing against Thérèse and Laurent? Hasn't friendship certain obligations? Bibi had said Thérèse trusted her. And like all women she had added that it meant a lot to her. Ah, to recall the way Thérèse nodded at La Motte-Picquet when I asked her to greet Bibi! It was true that Thérèse was alone. She herself said she had been alone until Bibi came to work for her mother, and naturally the great event of her life was my coming into the nineteenth of her nineteen years, a very young age, an age at which the future should be full of hope. Not so in Thérèse's case. Her future was were false hopes; and that, the work of those very people—including myself—who were supposed to love her with a love that had no limits. Perhaps this couldn't be applied to Bibi. But she was Thérèse's friend and she had told me that she and I were the only real friends Thérèse had; that she knew how Thérèse felt about her parents. But was it right?

Not that I thought all that as I was on Bibi. One doesn't think when one is on a woman at the peak of excitement. One sinks and withdraws and sinks and does not think and withdraws; sinks and turns, thrusts and withdraws; quicker now; quick, rhythmically, breathing, hard; she too breathes hard. One sinks and withdraws and doesn't think … Bibi!

We washed ourselves and got dressed.

We locked the room and went downstairs. Thérèse and Laurent were in Paris. But also Thérèse's parents. Bibi and I couldn't go and take the Métro at the Ecole Militaire. Supposing we were seen by Laurent? Or by Thérèse's mother, in her car, or her father, in his, as we walked along the Avenue de la Motte-Picquet to go to the Métro? Thérèse's trust meant a lot to Bibi. As for me, to be seen with Bibi on Bibi's afternoon off would certainly create trouble. Such news could destroy Thérèse. So the best thing to do was to call a taxi to pick us up at the door of the hotel.

I asked the receptionist to please telephone for a taxi. She said:

'Très bien, monsieur …'

Bibi and I went into the lounge to wait.

Two young ladies sat opposite us, turning the pages of *The Week in Paris*. They weren't so young. They looked thirty and twenty-six. They looked both chaste and wayward, both of them.

'They're English,' Bibi whispered into my ear. Bibi had lived in England for a year, in London. She had returned to Stockholm before coming to Paris three years later. She had come to Paris to forget an affair which had led to a child. She loved Paris. She preferred it a thousand times to Stockholm. Perhaps that was why she wanted Laurent to marry her. She wanted to live the rest of her life in Paris, with an artist husband. But perhaps those weren't her intentions. It was Thérèse who said she thought Bibi wanted Laurent to marry her. But then, like me, Thérèse sometimes had too much imagination.

Now one of the two ladies, the one who looked twenty-six, said:

'Excuse me, do you speak English?'

'Yes,' I said.

She glanced at her friend; then looking at me again, she said:

'What interesting place can you advise us to go to? Or are you also strangers?'

'Not exactly,' I said. 'An interesting place?'

'Yes,' she smiled and glanced at her friend; then looking away from the woman who looked thirty—she was very pretty—she said: 'We're strangers. It's the first time we've been in Paris and we don't speak a word of French.'

They both smiled. The one who had spoken to us even laughed.

I turned to Bibi; our eyes met. Bibi smiled.

'It depends on what you want?' I said, looking at the two tourists.

They both shrugged their shoulders.

'Oh, anything nice,' the twenty-six-year-old one said, assuming that was her age. She wasn't as pretty as her friend. She had a round face and a rather thick chin. And she was thicker, with a bosom whereas her friend didn't seem to have one. She—the one who looked thirty—was very slim and her eyes were very pretty; they were more than that. They were calm with a kind of healthy melancholy in them. She wasn't very talkative. In fact she said nothing to us until later.

'We intend going out ourselves,' I said. 'We're waiting for a taxi. Perhaps you could join us. We want to have dinner then we could go to a night club, something quite modest but nice. So if that programme suits you, we'd be your guides tonight. Eh, Bibi?'

Naturally, she couldn't say no.

'Yes,' Bibi said, looking good-naturedly at the two women.

'Well thanks,' the younger of the two women said after

consulting the pretty one with a look. 'That's very nice of you.'

The receptionist announced that the taxi was at the door.

'So here we are,' I said, rising. 'The taxi's outside.'

We let the two women walk in front of us. The pretty one was slim. She was Thérèse's height. The younger one, who wasn't pretty, was shorter than me by a couple of inches. She was thick but not as thick as Bibi. Not that Bibi was very thick and ugly. No. Bibi was big and beautiful. She was a bit taller than me. But it didn't matter.

Outside, I opened the door of the taxi. The women got in, and I told the driver to take us to a certain restaurant on the Left Bank, not far from the Ecole Nationale Superieure Des Beaux Arts. I gave him the name of the street and the number.

The Paris of cafés, right and left; the Paris of traffic lights and curses—not always—the Paris of pretty steps on the pavement. Two young ladies laughing in front of a shop-window, gossiping perhaps about Jean-Jacques or Emile and Irène or Sidonie and their flirtations or loves or divorces. Paris. The Paris of traffic lights—red, yellow and green—and neon lights; green crosses for pharmacies.

The wind was fresh; I had almost said the wind was French! It beat against the window of the car with an urgent but nevertheless guarded friendliness and I thought of Thérèse.

More traffic lights. More people on the pavements.

The Paris of art galleries The Paris of artists and art critics and intellectuals, bearded and unbearded. The *Café Flore. Aux Deux Magots.* And that aged clock on the Church in the Place de Saint Germain des Prés.

The Paris of students. But most of them had gone away for the summer holidays. The Paris of tourists.

The taxi drew up outside the restaurant. The women got out. I paid the taxi driver and tipped him. I got out and banged the door, hard. I was happy in spite of Thérèse who had begun again to intervene in my thoughts.

As the taxi drove off and I joined Bibi and the two tourists, the younger one wanted to know how much they owed me.

'Nothing, my dear,' I said, casually. 'We would have taken a taxi anyway and the fare would have been the same.'

'Oh, thanks!' she said as if surprised.

'Let's go in,' I said.

We entered the softly-lit restaurant. I had dined with Thérèse there; three times. Twice on my own initiative; and the third on hers, and it was she who had paid on that occasion. It was like that between Thérèse and I. She paid when it was she who had invited me; and I paid when it was I who had asked her out.

The restaurant. Naked light mellowed by red bulbs which shone from low walls. A record was on. A place for all appetites!

'Romantic!' I heard the younger girl say under her breath.

That was true. In the same place, months ago I had talked to Luisa of the music of days of hope, music of the dusk with winds of the future and gypsies telling stories to guitars and stars, waiting for the dawn and death. And the literature student from Barcelona had said how *romantico* I was!

And now this girl with a round, not so pretty face had suddenly been put in the mood for romance. That was Paris. A writer lives the city, feels it, observes it as he observes himself, lives his life, feeling; and his mind processes the memories according to the internal impulses that animate and re-animate his life. As far as I was concerned, those impulses gave my life the following pattern: a refusal to side with oppression or repression. Then there was that melancholy that couldn't however interfere with hope, which is creation. And then desire. But few people understood me for they snatched at the things I said and failed to see that art wasn't only on paper or in wood, metal, marble or stone. It was also in the air and hence it could be on the tongue. And art was deeper than the depths to which many people cared to penetrate in their search for significance and beauty. I wrote because it came to me naturally and writing seemed to me to be a magnificent experience; especially reading over what one has written! Thérèse believed so much in my writing; which, possibly, was *one* of the reasons why I decided to marry her. I could reveal to her the things I thought she needed and which luckily she could appreciate. I used to tell her that when I was sixty I'd write very good books. She said she wanted to read them before she died and she didn't intend to live to be sixty, as if it were something one could arrange for oneself. She said the ceiling she was giving herself was forty years. *Grand maximum.* She didn't want to grow old. She said death was better than old age.

'So you'll have to hurry up with your books,' she had said.

'But there's still time,' I had replied, 'plenty of time between now and your *grand maximum*—'

She had smiled.

'You're making fun of me,' she had said, nudging me.

'No. Why? There's still time. The books will come.'

'I'm waiting for them,' she said encouragingly.

The restaurant. Drums and a flute and maracas rose from the record that was being played at the bar. Two men were perched on high stools, the type that made eyes at women and ran away with them a week or so later—other people's women—to pleasure resorts. The two men talked to the barman, a tall fellow in a white jacket who looked very sober.

As soon as the younger of the two tourists had declared under her breath that the place was romantic, a man in a black suit walked up to us with a big smile.

'For four?' he asked, twisting a napkin in his hands.

'Yes, please,' I replied.

And he led us to a table in the far end of the restaurant.

People looked at us because I was alone with three women.

The record at the bar was a bolero.

I thought of Thérèse.

Chapter Twelve

As soon as we sat down we introduced each other. That was on the initiative of the younger of the two tourists. She told Bibi and me that they were nurses. She was Mary. The slim, pretty one who looked older was Dora. She was serene, reserved, profound.

Mary was direct, plain, talkative. It was she who said they wanted something typically French for dinner.

We wasted a lot of time over the menu because of Mary and Dora. Mary would put a finger on an item and then ask for the translation in English. Bibi and I did the explaining. Laughter. Mary liked to laugh. She would laugh and glance at Dora; then she would point to another item on the menu. Dora would smile. Bibi or I would translate the item Mary was pointing at. It was funny that she seemed to find the dishes which were catalogued on the menu amusing. She would listen to our translation and then she would turn excitedly to her friend, and then she would laugh. She was touchingly happy. But Dora remained cool. She answered Mary in an almost inaudible voice. I liked her. Dora's eyes were lovely and discreet. She looked dignified even though I felt there was something tentative about her.

The waitress came three times. Each time we said we weren't ready. Mary would look up at the woman; then, lowering her eyes to the menu, she would laugh. Perhaps it was because she was in Paris that site was so happy. The city did that to some women. Very curiously, before withdrawing, the waitress said: *'Très bien.'*

When she came for the fourth time we were ready. It was Bibi who told her what we wanted. Mary and Dora went for soup; I for a green salad. Bibi, nothing for the first course … . Red wine. Mineral water. Mary and Bibi and Dora drank the red wine while I drank the mineral water. I don't think the two nurses who had asked for the wine were used to drinking red wine at meals. But they were in Paris and they had said they wanted a typically French dinner, which was natural, being tourists. And wine was one of those things that really nationalize meals in France.

The second course: *escalope* for the two nurses; *rôti de veau* for Bibi and *côte de pore* for me.

Dessert: ice-cream—Champigny—for Mary, Dora and Bibi; an apple for me.

After dinner I proposed our going to the night club I had mentioned to them at the hotel. Mary was immediately enthusiastic. Dora wasn't so carried away by the idea. One would have said she hadn't heard of it before whereas at the hotel Mary had consulted her with a look when I had talked of the dinner-night-club programme.

At the Club there were many young people. That meant jokes and laughter and cries. The girls laughed loudest, perpetually amused by the boys who seemed to be making great efforts to entertain the girls as if the jazz wasn't enough.

The drums and trumpets and sax and piano and bass and clarinet.

Lovely.

People danced. Others only listened to the jazz; quite a few neither danced nor listened to the music. One could see they weren't listening, like the boys and girls who talked and laughed and played.

We sat down.

The night club was in a cellar. It was like a country baker's red-brick oven, but more spacious. It wasn't very stuffy. There were electric fans. They helped. The jazz wasn't bad.

Mary went into the arms of the first man who asked her for a dance. Dora kept on refusing to dance. No thank you. More than four people came to ask her. No thank you.

A fellow in a dark suit, with the cuffs of his shirt reaching almost to his knuckles, strode over to our table. His collar was also very prominent. A dandy, and he was handsome. He asked Bibi to dance with him.

'No thank you,' said Bibi, in French.

'You're sure you don't want to dance?' he asked. '*C'est vrai?*' 'Yes,' Bibi smiled.

'It won't hurt you, a dance,' said the man. 'Come and dance.'

'Non merci.'

'Or is it because of monsieur …' He glanced at me. 'He won't be angry. *Allez* come. Be nice.'

'You bore me,' Bibi said.

I simply liked that.

'Mais voyons,' the man with the prominent collar and shirt cuffs almost reaching his knuckles insisted.

I thought he was a very shy fellow in spite of his little show of boldness, the kind of man who asks a woman to dance and, when refused, doesn't know how to return to his seat. So he remained on the spot and tried to talk because it was the easier thing to do; going back, refused, was more humiliating—to his type—and so he remained before the woman, talking, insisting, knowing very well that nothing would come out of it.

'Listen, Bibi,' I said. 'Dance if you feel like dancing.'

Bibi didn't say anything. She folded her arms under her bosom—she had pretty large breasts, Bibi—and looked away.

Now the fellow moved away.

I asked Dora for a dance. She got up and we began to dance not far from our table. She danced well, Dora. A Blues. Her body was tender. She was so slim.

'You dance very well,' I said.

'Do I?' she asked, head backwards, as she looked into my face.

'True,' I nodded.

'Thanks,' she said.

When we returned to our seats Dora offered Bibi a cigarette. Bibi smiled and declined. Dora then held the packet to me. I told her I didn't smoke. She took one herself, placed it between her lips and turned to her right and began searching in her handbag.

A box of matches. She scratched one; the flame. She lowered her cigarette to it and its end was soon golden, burning—a tiny fragrant fire-brand.

She shook her right hand from the wrist, putting out the match-stick flame. She dropped it in the ashtray, shut her handbag, replaced it on the floor, by her feet, and sat up; then she leaned back, her head tilted even further backwards, her eyes turned to the arched roof of the dance cave.

Mary returned with the man she had been dancing with. She introduced him. He was Mustapha. She introduced us to him. I helped Mary with my name, then with Bibi's, reminding her of them. Yes. Doumbe, Bibi. Mustapha sat with us. He was putting on weight. He wasn't particularly handsome. He looked tough. Mary's face was all red.

Mustapha offered Mary a cigarette. She accepted. He offered one to Bibi. She declined. Mustapha then held the packet to me. I said thanks without taking the trouble to explain that I didn't smoke. Mustapha lit Mary's cigarette. He spoke some English.

The band was playing a quick number.

Mary and Mustapha and Dora smoked and we talked. Bibi was detached. Her long nose looked longer; her round cheeks, more rounded and fuller. Her large eyes were sad. But she nevertheless looked pretty in an ample sort of way, the kind of woman who could have made a wonderful match for the visiting head of a government. A woman whose imposing features made her suitable for visits to children's hospitals and places like that while her husband discussed affairs of state with his official hosts.

The quick number ended; something happened to the lights, something deliberate. They mellowed and the band struck up another blues.

Mustapha thumbed his cigarette in the ash-tray and coarsely tugged at Mary's hand. They went to dance. A very young man asked Dora for a dance. She left her cigarette in the ashtray and went to dance.

I turned to Bibi.

'Let's dance,' I said.

'No,' she mumbled, without even looking at me. 'I don't feel like dancing.'

'What then do you feel like doing?' I asked, irascibly.

'I don't know,' she said rather sulkily.

'Listen, come and dance.'

'No!'

'Listen, I'll be angry.'

'Then what are you waiting for?' she barked. 'Go ahead, get angry.'

'Bibi.'

'What?'

'What's the matter?'
'Nothing.'
'Laurent?'
'Oh, shut up!'
'Why?'
'Listen, can't I be left alone?'
'Is it about Dora?'
'Dora!'
'Yes.'
'Why?'
'Maybe because I danced with her.'
'Nonsense.'
I felt like slapping her, but I controlled myself.
She rose.
'Where are you going?'
'I'm leaving.'
'Okay. I'll meet you at the hotel.'
'I'm not going to the hotel.'
I got up.
'Bibi, tell me. What's wrong?'
'I've told you, nothing.'
'Then why are you sulking?'
She began to move away. 'Good night,' she said.
'Let's at least say good-bye to Dora and her friend. We won't be seeing them again.'
'You don't have to come with me. I'm not going to the hotel.'

'Then where are you going?'

'Home.'

She turned her back on me.

I watched her walk to the foot of the steps that led to the ground-floor and the street.

Chapter Thirteen

MUSTAPHA took Mary to his place.
Dora and I returned to the hotel in a taxi.

Outside the door of her room we said good night to each other in spite of the dawn.

It was the chambermaid's knock on the door of my room that woke me up. The sun and the pigeons were outside the window.

'Are you keeping the room for the day?' she asked from the other side of the door.

'No,' I replied and yawned.

'*Bon*,' she said, 'you'll have to surrender the key before midday.'

'Okay.'

She had heavy footfalls; they pounded their way down the corridor and I heard her knock on the next door. I had only a fortnight more to be in Europe. It was strange that Thérèse hadn't pressed for arrangements for our marriage to be hastened. Perhaps she thought about it; but she had her pride. I had had to talk of the embassy two days ago for her to agree with me that it was time things got started.

After dressing, I packed my travelling bag and went down stairs. I gave the key to the flame-lipped receptionist and went out into the mid-July sunshine.

I took the Métro at the Ecole Militaire and went to the Latin Quarter; had lunch there, before returning to Madame Bistrott's.

A letter from my father was waiting for me on the table. Madame Bistrott had put it there.

My father said he had transferred money to me. He hoped I had received it by now. About my fiancée, he wrote, he had no objections provided the girl loved me. My mother had hesitated; but she too was now agreed and was looking forward to seeing her white daughter-in-law … It was a severe rainy season. The floods were unprecedented. One of his canoes had been swept away by the water. He had sent people to the south, to look for it … Didn't I think I should delay my return? A white woman would find the rainy season most difficult to bear. Couldn't I delay my return until November or December when the water would have left the forest? He didn't say when the water would have left the forest. He said when the water had gone down; that is, subsided. But perhaps, he said, I should come as planned, at the end of the month. If my wife was going to live with us she might as well begin by going through the rainy season now.

Then he said I should greet my future parents-in-law for him. He said I should tell them that the West was far away; but in the heart there were no distances.

When I had finished reading the letter I went out. I entered the café which was on the other side of the street and telephoned.

It was Bibi who answered the phone. I ignored the fact that it was the erratic Bibi of last night, the Bibi who had always been nice until last night. I ignored her and simply asked if I could speak to Madame Vaele.

'Doumbe?' Bibi asked.

'Yes. Can I speak to Madame Vaele?'

Silence. Then she said:

'Doumbe—'

'Listen, Bibi. Can I speak to Madame Vaele?'

'Yes,' she said, but she seemed to be holding on, for I didn't hear the receiver being put on the piece of furniture on which the telephone stood.

I knew she wanted to talk to me; but she couldn't. What had happened last night, like all that had been happening between us, had to remain a secret to the Vaele family.

'Bibi!'

'Hold on.'

I heard her leave the receiver on the table or whatever it was on which the telephone stood; a console table perhaps.

After a while I heard faint footsteps; then the receiver was lifted.

'Who is speaking?'

'Doumbe.'

'*Oh, bonjour.* How are you?'

'Not very well. Is your husband at home?'

'No.'

'And Thérèse?'

'She's in her room. You want me to call her?'

'No. Listen, madame. Be careful the way you reply. And tell Bibi not to tell Thérèse that I telephoned. It is very delicate, all that. Are you listening?'

'Yes.'

'Very good. Listen and reply by yes or no.'

'Go on.'

'I want to discuss Thérèse with you, very urgently. And not even her father should know about this telephone call. We are in trouble, Thérèse and I, and it's only you who can help us. I love Thérèse. That's why I'm telephoning. I want to discuss something very important with you—'

'A child?'

'Psh. Be discreet, please. No. It's not about a child.'

But perhaps she was right; how was I to know? It was Friday. But by Monday or Tuesday, I'd know. However that wasn't what I wanted to discuss with her.

'Go on then,' she said, relieved.

'Can I see you at the Drug Store in the Champs Elysées at four, that is in a hour's time.'

'Some other place perhaps.'

'The café of the other day? You remember? Where Thérèse introduced you to me.

'Yes.'

'You think you'll be able to find it?'

'Yes.'

'Okay. Four o'clock. Will that suit you?'

'Yes.'

'I'm very glad you've accepted. It's very important.'

'So long then.'

'Yes, so long.'

The sun was a wan yellow over the Seine and the bridge and the buildings on the other side of the river.

The waiter asked me what I would drink. I ordered ice-cream for although it was shady on the terrace it was far from cool. It was a very hot summer.

The sun was still on the terrace of a rival café on the right of the cross-roads. Traffic was heavy at the cross-roads. The terrace of the other café was more crowded than the one on which I was. People even sat outside, on the pavement, under parasols. They looked somnolent. A number of them must have been tourists like Dora and Mary.

The waiter returned with my ice-cream. I was eating it when I saw the tall figure of Madame Vaele appear from the road comer. She smiled when she saw me and walked a bit faster. Eyes were turned to her as she walked towards my table. I felt a bit embarrassed. It must have been equally embarrassing for her.

I rose from my chair and we shook hands.

'You look a bit tired,' she observed.

'Nothing serious,' I said, drawing up a chair for her.

She sat down. Her eyes were particularly brilliant that afternoon; almost like healthy youthful eyes. Her blouse was open at the neck and I saw how bony she was below the neck which was Thérèse's neck, long. But it was strange that Thérèse had hips while her mother hadn't, not to talk of the backside where Madame Vaele was flat. It wasn't strange! It was amazing. But nature is like that. Madame Vaele's eyes were nice in spite of the wrinkles at their corners. The two folds or wrinkles down either side of her face, from the comers of her nose to the comers of her mouth which had been so prominent the first day I saw her were less prominent today. It seemed she had been sleeping better since it was agreed that I could marry Thérèse; she had resigned herself to the fact. That must be why her face looked less strained, less tormented.

'*Alors*,' she smiled, genially. 'What is this important and delicate thing you want to discuss?'

It was surprising how she had resisted the anxiety which my alarmist telephone call would normally have occasioned her—she who was said to be so weak. She was so gay. I later thought that perhaps it was because Thérèse wasn't there; for it's rare for a woman to be herself in the presence of her daughter and her daughter's lover, or even her daughter's fiancé. A girl in such circumstances easily mistakes gaiety for coquetry. And jealousy soon becomes spite.

'First of all,' I began, 'I'd like to know if you really are in agreement with my marrying Thérèse and my taking her to Africa.'

'To tell the truth,' Thérèse's mother said, looking me in the eyes, her head tilted a bit to the left, 'I was against it. It's normal. But now that I know Thérèse really loves you, I have come to accept it with all my heart. It's not the colour of one's skin that matters. What people look for is happiness. Since she feds she will be happy with you, I, as her mother, cannot but accept her choice. You see?'

'I think I see, madame,' I said.

'At first we were afraid, Thérèse and I, because it seemed you had never told her that you loved her.'

'Yes?'

'At least the word love. You don't seem to have pronounced it to her—'

'It's possible. But now it's different.'

'She will be very glad to know it.'

'Glad?'

'Yes. She was worried.'

We fell silent. Thérèse's mother gazed at the table, her fingers playing with the bit of paper on which the pricing machine had printed the cost of the ice-cream. I didn't think she saw that bit of paper she was turning with her fingers on the table. Her thoughts must have been far away; in Africa, for example, the Africa her husband knew and which, if things worked out well, Thérèse would soon know but which she would never know; for her doctors had advised her against setting foot in the tropics. Yes her neck was Thérèse's neck, long; but Thérèse's was youthful and more beautiful. I had told Ndome that it was a swan's neck, a crane's neck, which to us is a way of praising a woman's neck. Not that we praise them very often. But from time to time one says something like that with a little exaggeration which gives the effect of subtle irony.

Madame Vaele sighed.

The waiter came to our table and asked:

'What will madame have to drink?'

'Pine-apple juice,' she said after a little hesitation.

I had told Thérèse two days ago that I'd wait for her at home at five.

'What time is it?' I asked her mother. I hadn't a wristwatch.

'Four-fifteen,' she said.

I thanked her and looked discreetly about me. The eyes which had been turned towards us when she had entered were now minding their business and with them, the ears. No one seemed any longer to be taking an interest in my presence on the terrace with a tall, ageing woman.

She was served with the pine-apple juice. She thanked the waiter who withdrew. Before Madame Vaele began to drink she opened her handbag. She took her purse from it and opening the purse she thrust two fingers into it. They came out with a fifty franc note which she put on the table. She shut the purse and replaced it in the handbag which she put under the table.

'I was going to pay,' I said.

She smiled. 'It doesn't matter,' she said.

Some three minutes passed during which she drank half her glass. Now she sat back, licked her lips which were thinner than Thérèse's and looked about her.

The waiter came and took the money she had put on the table. From the inside pocket of his jacket he took a purse which was loaded with notes. He opened it and added the fifty franc note to the others. Then he counted out the change—four ten-franc notes which he put on the table. He dipped his hand in the side pocket of his jacket. It came out with some coins a number of which he put on the table.

Madame Vaele took the change and left a franc for the waiter's tip. The man thanked her and went to take the order of a young lady who had just entered the café and was seating herself at a table.

'Thérèse said she's seeing you at five,' Madame Vaele said.

'Yes.'

'We asked her to invite you home to lunch with us. We were thinking of sometime next week. Which day would suit you best?'

'Any day.'

'Wednesday?'

'Let's say Friday. Will that suit you?'

'Perfectly.'

I made a note of it in my pocket book.

'However,' I said, feeling I could now quietly acquaint her with what she still didn't know, 'I'll discuss it with Thérèse. It will be she who will tell you if I can come or not. And remember don't let her know we have seen each other.'

'But why?'

'Because her father doesn't want us to get married. He is wildly against it.'

'That's not true. Who told you, Thérèse?'

'No. Your husband himself. You remember he dined out about a week after his return from Abidjan last month.'

'I can't remember—'

'*Si*. He dined out; and it was with me. We discussed Thérèse and he confessed he was against it. Only he's afraid of Thérèse, her reaction. So he doesn't want her to know. He doesn't want her to know that he is behind my letting her down.'

'Because you are going to let her down?'

'That is what your husband is asking me to do. His idea is that I should say I'm going ahead. That Thérèse should follow me, at least that is what we'd make her believe. I guess he hopes that once I am away she'll forget me.'

'I can't believe it.'

'It's true. That's what I wanted to discuss with you.'

'It's impossible.'

'But there's a solution—'

'What?'

'First, don't discuss it with him, or you may, if you want; but only in a round-about way. And above all Thérèse mustn't know what is going on—'

'It's hard to believe.'

'Indeed. And then knowing that my parents have given their consent; not that I needed it legally. I'm twenty-three.'

'Have they written?'
'Yes; this very day.'
She sighed; then she mused:
'Jacques wouldn't do that—'
'He's done it. So go and think it over. I'll telephone you on Monday, around ten o'clock. If you're ready to give us your consent, as soon as you hear my voice, simply say "yes". If you side with your husband, simply say "no". You know that legally your consent is as good as yours and his put together. The consent of one of the parents is enough. So all our hopes are in your saying "yes". If you also don't want it, say no to me on Monday. In that case I'll carry out you,' husband's plan which seems to me the only reasonable one in the circumstances. The thing is to spare Thérèse any suffering. With only a fortnight left before my departure you can imagine how she's already wondering what will happen. She doesn't talk to me about it, or ask me what I have done so far about the marriage; and I suppose she's not been asking you about it either. She's a girl, still very young and although she may not confess it, Thérèse has a lot of pride. She's already suffering, secretly, at the fact that not even the engagement has been celebrated and yet I have only a fortnight left.'

'I was also wondering what was happening. At home we rarely mention the subject with the exception of yesterday when Jacques asked Thérèse to invite you for lunch. I exaggerate. We talk about it, from time to time, but not in detail.'

'You said it was he who asked that I be invited?'

'Yes. That's why I don't understand.'

'However, you go and think over what I have just told you. Should you also decide to withhold your consent, then we shall have to find an opportune occasion to inform Thérèse that we can't go together. Thérèse would remain with you and she'll forget me after a few months.'

'And you?' Madame Vaele asked, tears in her eyes.

'I too will learn to forget. What she will have I'll have: distance and time.'

I found Thérèse waiting for the lift. I kissed her on the cheek.

'How was it at the embassy yesterday?' she asked.

'The usual thing: wait, wait,' I lied. I had to. I couldn't tell her that I hadn't been to the embassy; that I had spent the afternoon with Bibi at a hotel, and had made the acquaintance of two nurses: Dora and Mary. I couldn't tell her all that; or I could have told her; but such moral heroism would have perhaps exalted me while there was no doubt that it would have ruined her. Her hopes were false hopes; but they helped her continue to live more or less happily.

'What did they say?' she asked.

The lift landed.

'Listen, Thérèse, let's have a walk instead of going to my room. It must be very stuffy up there.'

'D'accord.'

We went out.

'What did you do yesterday?'

'Nothing special … But you haven't told me what they said at the embassy.'

'They said they couldn't give me any document to replace my birth certificate. You know we'll need it. Yours also, for the Registry.'

'I've got mine.'

'I have never seen mine. The Consul-General said he would write home. I should wait.'

'But shall we have time?'

'I don't know … You look ill.'

'It's nothing.'

'Are you sure?'

'Yes.'

'Is it your period?'

'Yes.'

'But that's rather early.'

'More or less.'

Very good, I thought, with great relief. There was no point in leaving her with a child. Bibi had had to leave hers in Stockholm and, according to Thérèse, she thought of the baby a lot. I didn't want to go away and think all the time of a child who would never know its father; a son or daughter I'd never know.

'How's Bibi?'

'There's news.'

'Tell me …'

'Laurent has proposed to her.'

'No!'
'It's true.'
'When?'
'Apparently two weeks ago.'
'Is she accepting?'
'I don't think so.'
'But why?'
'Perhaps because she doesn't love him.'
'Was it Bibi who told you?'
'Who else could have told me?'
'Formidable!'

'She's been thinking it over for two weeks. She still hasn't given him her reply. She wants time to think it over.'

'What's the point in taking so long to say yes or no? It's stupid to keep him in suspense,' I said.

'It's a veritable suspense,' Thérèse chorused. 'She's not even been seeing him since.'

'That I didn't know.'

'Nor did I.'

'That's cowardly. Why not tell him straight away that she doesn't want him?'

'I don't know; and it looks as though she's been seeing someone else.'

'Ah?'

'She was away the whole of yesterday afternoon—'

'Wasn't that her day off?'

'Yes. But look at the time she came home?'

'When did she come home?'

'Around 1 a.m.'

'How did you know?'

'I was awake *voyons*! I heard her come in.'

'And you're sure it wasn't from Laurent's place that she was coming.'

'Yes. I talked to her this afternoon. I noticed she's been a bit moody, for some time now really; so I wanted to talk to her. Whenever I feel depressed myself it's she who tries to cheer me up. I tried to do the same for her. This afternoon, after lunch, I followed her to her room and tried to make her talk.'

'What did she say?'

'She said she was going through a crisis.'

'We all are—'

'But hers is acute. According to her she doesn't know how to tell Laurent that she doesn't want to see him any more.'

'And you say there's another boy?'

'Apparently, but she didn't talk to me about it. She only told me that Laurent had proposed to her and that she didn't know what to tell him, and in fact didn't even want to see him …'

'But you said she's not going to accept him.'

'Yes. That's what she doesn't know how to tell him. You see she doesn't want him to suffer.'

'Why should he suffer?'

'It's normal that it would make him suffer.'

'I've been very worried about Bibi recently.'

'Yes?'
'Yes.'
'How?'
'Since we were going to get married—'
'Were?'
'I mean since we are going to get married I've thought she's been feeling jealous.'

'I don't think so.'

'She may not have shown it but it always happens that when two girls are going out with two boy friends, as soon as two of them are going to get married, the girl whose boy still hasn't proposed marriage feels jealous. Her boy feels uneasy. That must explain, at least in part, Laurent's proposal. Bibi must have told him about us.'

'Certainly.'

'What surprises me is that she is refusing. You once said she would like to be his wife.'

'She implied it in what she said. She wanted to find a job so as to be able to help him. She thought he was a talented painter and she wanted him to succeed. One of her problems was how to tell him that she had a child.'

'Life is difficult.'

'I know.'

'It's not easy at all.'

We walked into a public park.

'I forgot to tell you—'

'What?'

'Mother wants you to come to the house for lunch.'

'That's very nice of her.'
'Which day will suit you?'
'What is today?'
'Friday.'
'Sometime next week.'
'Why not earlier?'
I sat down on a bench. Thérèse also sat down.
'I'll be busy.'
'Doing what?'
'I'll be busy—isn't that enough?'
She sighed.

It was a small park with a church. Old women sat on the benches, some on chairs, sunning themselves. The sunshine was soft. It was evening. But the sun is never in a hurry to set in summer. There were also a few old men, left-overs from the war and other misfortunes. They sat on the benches, their eyes closed. Children with plastic pails and shovels and even rakes played on a mound of sand. A few young ladies were also in the park. Some sat near prams which they rocked. Others, legs crossed, knitted. Some old women also knitted.

'So what day next week?'
'Friday.'
'What about an affidavit?' she suddenly said, after a brief silence? "People can get married with an affidavit if it's impossible for them to produce birth certificates."

She was a victim of all of us, as well as a victim of many things, including our lies. But the terrible thing was that we all thought we were acting in her interest—at least as far as keeping things secret from her was concerned. As she had said, Bibi didn't want Laurent to suffer just as we did not want her to suffer.

'An affidavit?'

'Yes.'

'I think that's what I'll have to do.'

'You'd better hurry up if we are to leave by the end of the month. I can't understand how we've let all the time pass without doing anything.'

'Two weeks are enough.'

'If we begin from now. The publicity at the registry is for ten days, isn't it?'

'Yes.'

Chapter Fourteen

NDOME, the African girl, invited me to a party on Sunday. The boy she called her fiancé wasn't there. I don't even know if she had a fiancé. But she said she had one. However, he wasn't at the party for she would have introduced him to me.

Besides myself, there were five other African boys; and there was Ndome and three other girls. We talked about Africa and we danced. Ndome told everybody that I was going to marry a white woman. The girls booed me. The boys were indifferent.

'Eh, you are going to do that kind of thing?' one of the girls asked, the backs of her hands on her hips.

'Yes,' I said.

A very slim girl came to me and took hold of one of my ears. 'How many times must you be told to leave white women alone?' she asked, pulling my ear. She was speaking into my ear. 'How many times?'

I raised my face and looked at her. Her eyes were frank, nice and passionate.

'A woman is a woman,' one of the boys said.

'Exactly,' another boy chorused. 'We aren't racists.'

'That's right,' Ndome sneered. 'You're not racists.'

'You keep on disgracing your sisters,' one of the girls said.

'Haven't you seen African girls with white boys?' a boy asked.

The obvious reply would have been that a man was a man irrespective of the colour of his skin. But the girls said nothing of that nature.

'How many girls, African girls,' one of them asked, 'went with white men? Eh, tell me, how many?'

'Leave them,' Ndome said. 'Doumbe is taking his own to Africa; that thing! You should have seen her hips …

I let them talk. I couldn't or didn't want to list my problems with Thérèse's father for debate. I was almost sure the girls would have sided with Monsieur Vaele.

I returned from the party very late and went to bed around two in the morning.

When I woke up, it was already half past ten. Monday. I thought of Thérèse's mother. I had promised her on Friday that I'd ring up around ten … I recalled my conversation with Thérèse. The affidavit. The registry.

I got out of bed, wound the clock on the mantelpiece and went into the bathroom.

I went to the café on the other side of our street, wondering what Thérèse's mother's reply would be. Would she make it possible for us to get married? Would she make it possible for me to take Thérèse to Africa at the end of the month? Or would she deny us her consent?

I lifted the receiver and dialled their number.

It was Bibi who answered the phone.

'Madame Vaele,' I said.

'Doumbe?' Bibi asked.

'Yes. I want to speak to Madame.'

I heard the breath of Bibi's silence.

'Doumbe.'

'Yes?'

'I'm sorry about Thursday.'

'Psh!'

'It doesn't matter. I'm alone.'

'Where's Madame Vaele?'

'She's gone out.'

'And Thérèse?'

'She went out with Madame.'

'And her father?'

'He's at his office.'

'Okay. I'll ring up again.'

'Doumbe.'

'What's the matter?'

'Honestly I'm sorry about my leaving you the way I did on Thursday. I don't know what came over me. Perhaps I was simply tired. I'm sorry.'

'It's all right. When did you say Madame Vaele will be back?'

'I don't know. In an hour's time perhaps.'

'Okay. I'll ring up again—'

'Doumbe.'

'Yes?'

'When can I see you?'

'Listen, Bibi. We've been stupid enough, both of us. It's time we stopped all this nonsense. Go and see Laurent. He loves you. I'm sorry, but it's over.'

'Why?'

I hung up and left the telephone box. I climbed the steps from the basement. I had a coffee at the counter. Then I went to the bank, in the Latin Quarter. I found a queue. I joined it, reading a newspaper.

When it came to my turn I asked the girl behind the counter to see if funds had been transferred to me. She knew the number of my account by heart. She went to look. Once I had told her that it was incredible, the memory she had. I thought it was incredible because the bank had hundreds of clients who queued up along that counter every day. She had smiled and had raised her eyebrows, apparently in an effort to find a modest and effective explanation for the phenomenon. Finally she had said it was a matter of habit. Taxi drivers said the same thing when you asked them how they managed to know all the streets, alleys, avenues and boulevards in Paris and its suburbs. A matter of habit.

The girl who knew the number of my account by heart and even my name returned with a smile.

'Yes,' she said. 'Haven't you been written to?'

'No,' I said.

She shrugged her shoulders.

'That's strange,' she said.

She was very pretty and young, perhaps not as young as Thérèse; but she looked very young. Only her eyes were a bit big. But she was charming. She wore a green dress. She hadn't any overalls. But the girls who sat at the calculating machines wore overalls.

'Can I see the account?' I asked.

'Certainly,' she said and went to fetch it.

My father had transferred more than I had expected. There was enough for two fares—Paris-Tiko; it was clear he had thought of Thérèse. Papa wasn't a rich man, but that he had found the money filled me with a profound sense of gratitude.

That must have been from his savings. And he had thought of Thérèse! I knew how my parents loved me; and I knew how they were prepared to love my wife.

When I left the bank I telephoned M. Vaele's number again. Not at his office, the number of which I didn't know; but at his home.

'They aren't back yet,' said Bibi.

'Tell her mother that I'll wait for her at the café at four. And don't breathe a word about it to Thérèse.'

'I won't.'

'Very good.'

'But can't I see you, even for a few minutes?'

'I've told you, Bibi, that I haven't the time.'

'But you're seeing Madame?'

'That's different. It's about Thérèse. I love her and we

may still get married. I can't continue with you. Why can't you understand that?'

This time it was she who dropped the receiver before I could do so. I didn't like that at all.

At four o'clock Thérèse's mother found me waiting. I had arrived almost fifteen minutes earlier. She sat down. She looked tired and her eyes were ringed. I could see she had been crying.

'Well?' I asked.

She shook her head. 'I've tried to persuade him, but he doesn't want it.'

I knew she was concerned not so much about me as about the effect such a disappointment would have on Thérèse, how miserable it would make her.

'He doesn't want it?' I asked.

'No,' she shook her head. 'He doesn't want it. I said everything.'

'And you?'

Again she shook her head and tears welled up in her eyes.

'If I gave you my consent to make your marriage possible, that would be the end of mine,' she said, almost sobbing.

'I understood you were Catholics.'

'Yes.'

'Then how can your marriage break up?'

'He threatened me with a divorce.'

'Did he?'

'Yes.'

The tears ran down her cheeks. They made her look much younger.

She opened her handbag, found a handkerchief and wiped her eyes. We had attracted attention. A man and a woman and another man and another woman and a girl and another girl and an ageing man with an ageing woman were looking at us.

'Does Thérèse know?'

Madame Vaele shook her head. 'No,' she said, blowing her nose. 'She mustn't know.'

'What will monsieur and madame drink?' asked the waiter.

I didn't wait for Thérèse's mother to say what she wanted to drink.

'A coffee,' I said, 'and a pine-apple juice.'

Chapter Fifteen

WHEN we left the café, Thérèse's mother offered to give me a lift in her car. I declined but said I'd see her on Friday. The lunch to which they had invited me. She said all right.

I took the Métro and went to the Latin Quarter. I got off at Odéon, walked up the Rue de l'Ecole de Medicine and then crossed the Boulevard Saint Michel. I was going to the British Council Library in the Rue des Ecoles to read the latest issue of the review *West Africa*. But as I was passing the Café *Select Latin* I heard Laurent's voice. He was calling me. I turned and saw him. His long face with its sombre eyes, his bare forehead. He was alone, sitting under a parasol.

I went to his table.

'Sit down,' he said, 'or are you in a hurry?'

'No,' I said.

I drew up a chair and sat down. He asked me what I'd drink. I said a coffee. I didn't particularly want a coffee, but it was the cheapest thing one could ask for, and Laurent had very little money, at least the way I had known him. And since he had invited me, I knew he would insist on paying. So I asked for a coffee. He signalled for the waiter who soon came and took my order.

'I'm very sorry about the little incident at the dance,' he said. 'It's already a long time ago all that; but it's never too late to explain. I was only joking. I didn't think Thérèse would take it like that. She must be an extremely sensitive girl.'

'She is. But it doesn't matter.'

'It's true I was only joking—'

'I know ... Bibi told you Thérèse and I had decided to get married?'

'Yes. But her parents?'

'They're against it.'

'What will you do? You can wait until she's twenty-one.'

'I don't know—'

'But is it true that you're going back to Africa at the end of the month?'

'Yes.'

'So what will Thérèse do?'

'Nothing. What is there to do?'

'A pity.'

'And Bibi?'

He laughed. 'You've heard anything?'

'Thérèse told me you had proposed to her.'

'Bibi doesn't want me.'

'Has she told you so?'

'No. But since she doesn't even want to see me ...'

'Yes?'

'It's more than a fortnight since I saw her last. I've written. No reply.'

The waiter returned with my cup of coffee.

'Do take this thing away,' Laurent said to the waiter, pointing at the parasol. The waiter looked at the sky. The sun was no longer burning. So he folded the parasol. He could have folded it without having first to look at the sky; but he wanted to show us that he was free to appraise things for himself and then decide on whether or not to act as suggested. Something instinctive. But he took orders for coffee, tea, beer, fruit juice and a whole lot of things without having to appraise anything. No. Sometimes the orders were vague. A waiter asked for precisions, otherwise one was served and then said that wasn't what had been asked for. It might not be the waiter's fault. Having folded the parasol the waiter went into the café. We were virtually on the pavement.

I put a lump of sugar in the coffee and stirring it, I said:

'I understand Bibi's rather depressed these days.'

'Who told you, Thérèse?'

'Yes. Perhaps if you wrote to her again it would make her feel better.'

'Who? Bibi?'

'Yes.'

'No. I don't think I'll write. It's ridiculous when a girl doesn't want you—'

'I know.'

'Let her stay like that.'

'It depends on whether or not you love her.'

He frowned and looked away. 'I don't know,' he said, gloomily.

I thought perhaps if we went out dancing it would cheer him up. I wanted some distraction myself and there were girls. I thought of Dora and Mary. They weren't girls any longer. They were young women. But what was the difference? I thought of Dora and Mary again.

'What are you doing tonight?' I asked Laurent.

'Nothing special.'

'Let's go to a dance.'

'I don't like going to a dance without being accompanied.'

'I know two English girls. I can telephone them to see if they're free tonight.'

'Okay. What are they like?'

'Not bad.'

I went to the basement as soon as I had finished my cup of coffee. I telephoned. The receptionist said Dora and Mary weren't in. I left a message. I said I'd call at the hotel with a French friend of mine. Perhaps we could go out dancing. However I'd telephone again, between seven and seven-thirty.

We left the café at half-past five because I wanted to see that *West Africa*. So we went to the library. I shook hands with a couple of African friends and introduced Laurent in a whisper. Then I took the review and sat down and began to turn the pages. There was trouble here and there. That was what Thérèse's father had said he was afraid of. The situation in Africa. But the girl herself wasn't afraid. Love made the difference. Thérèse!

From the library—it closed at six—we went to the university restaurant which was open to cater for students who hadn't gone away on holidays, mostly those who had failed their exams in June and were reading, hard, nervously, against the autumn session. Carrots and cabbage and potatoes over which a piece of pork was put. That was the dinner. There were other things: salad and cake and cheese. One could ask for more vegetables if one was hungry. The restaurant wasn't very noisy. Noise and plenty of fun, laughter and pleasure may be responsible for a student's failure; but once he has failed, it is hard for him to continue to be noisy and gay. That certainly was the reason why the restaurant wasn't very noisy. It used to be very noisy before May.

After the meal I felt brighter, and even a little happy and Laurent's spirits seemed to have improved. I went and telephoned Dora.

She was in.

'Doumbe,' I said, 'how are you, Dora?'

'Fine, thank you. I got your note.'

'So?'

'Okay ... But I was wondering if we couldn't meet somewhere else, at the Métro?'

'Ecole Militaire—that's the nearest one.'

'Fine.'

'How's Mary?'

'She's with me. You want to say hello?'
'Yes.'

A word or two off the mouthpiece, inviting Mary to come and speak.

'How are you?'

'Fine, Mary. Are we seeing both of you tonight? I'll be with a friend of mine.'

'Yes.'

'How's Mustapha?'

'I haven't seen him since Friday.'

'Oh, yes?'

'He said he had work to do.'

'I see,' I said. I understood what had happened. He had made use of her and that was enough for him. Keep moving. One night was enough—and to think how red and happy Mary's face had been that night at the night club! That was what made so many girls bitter. 'Will you let Dora speak?'

'Certainly.'

'Dora?'

'Yes.'

'So it's fixed—Ecole Militaire. Eight-thirty.'

'All right.'

'At the ticket window.'

'Okay.'

Laurent was waiting for me outside.

'Did it work?'

'Yes. They'll wait for us at the Ecole Militaire, at eight-thirty.'

To while away the time I invited him to come and drink something in a café.

He asked for a coffee. I asked for a glass of mineral water. It came in a bottle. But it was exactly one glass.

We talked and when we weren't talking I thought about many things. I recalled Madame Vaele's face. The sincere eyes. 'If I give you my consent to make your marriage possible, that would be the end of mine!' That was what she had said.

But by the time Laurent and I left the café I was thinking of something else: supposing Dora and Mary suddenly began talking about Thursday night, talking about Bibi?

Dora and Mary were already at the Ecole Militaire when we arrived.

Dora looked prettier than she had done on Thursday night. Mary looked even less pretty and there was reason for her to look even less pretty. Mustapha had work to do. She must have known what that meant. There were rings under her eyes and her round face with its short upturned nose looked haggard in spite of her make-up.

'Dora, Mary,' I said, 'Laurent.'

They shook hands.

'Does he speak any English?' Mary asked.

'I speak English,' Laurent said with a smile.

'Oh, good,' Mary laughed. 'At least we can talk. Dora and I don't speak a single word of French.'

'That's not true,' Dora cut in, nicely, serenely, her head tilted sideways. 'I can say *bonjour*. You too.'

We all laughed. I noticed Dora was taking a discreet interest in Laurent. She sized him up from the corner of her eye and I thought she wanted him to notice it.

'So what do we do now?' asked Laurent. He seemed suddenly to have decided to impress the young ladies. That was very French.

'What have you in mind?' Mary inquired.

'Oh, nothing special,' he said, looking at me. There was friendly connivance in his eyes because we had decided we wouldn't go to the dance as I had suggested. We would take them to his place for a talk, music and coffee foursome. Marc's records were there.

'Why don't we surface,' I said, having decided that we mustn't rush things. 'We could sit in a café and make up our minds.'

'All right,' Mary agreed.

We went to the café. They had coffee, the three of them, and they smoked. I had a glass of cold milk. We talked about many things; but neither Dora nor Mary asked me about Bibi. The abrupt manner in which she left us at the club the other night.

Then Laurent said he was inviting us to listen to records at his place. He asked me what I thought as if we hadn't taken the decision together. I said it was okay with me. He asked Dora and Mary. Mary consulted the serene and lovely Dora with a look. Dora made a slight nod.

'Well, all right,' Mary said. 'We think we can trust you.'

We took the Métro and changed at La Motte-Picquet and soon we were at Place d'Italie.

When we got to the landing outside Laurent's door—it was Marc's really, but meanwhile it was Laurent's—Laurent searched his pockets for his keys, found them and opened the door. He turned on the light and we went in. To my horror there was Bibi's portrait on a canvas pinned to a board on Laurent's easel in the centre of the room.

'That's Laurent's fiancée,' I hurriedly remarked.

Dora and Mary exchanged looks.

'So he's a painter?' Dora asked without taking her eyes away from the painting. It was Bibi done with humility and devotion. Her large eyes, her broad face, the long nose, the rounded cheeks, the bosom. The emotion on her face was fear.

'Laurent's a painter,' I said, sitting down.

'I like it,' Dora said to Laurent with admiration in her eyes.

'I never knew he could paint that well already,' I said, sincerely. 'He's still at the Fine Arts School.'

'I didn't think I could do it either,' Laurent said, dropping into a chair. 'Do sit down—'

'Thanks,' said Mary, sitting down on the bed.

Dora remained standing, admiring the painting.

Laurent suddenly grew weary.

'I didn't think I could do it,' he said, 'at least not as seriously as that. But there it is. A work of one night. It's not finished you know. I am waiting for her to return. I've been waiting over two weeks.'

'She'll return,' Dora said compassionately and I knew she had understood what was happening. I knew she wouldn't talk of that night at the night club. 'Don't be sad.'

Laurent didn't reply. He closed his eyes. He had changed. He wasn't looking or behaving above his age as he used to do in the past. He looked frail and exhausted.

'Have you any others?' Dora asked.

'Yes, but they're no good,' he said. 'That's the first serious work I've done and it is unfinished.'

We later listened to records. Then when Mary put on a blues Laurent got up, to my surprise, smiled, and asked Dora to dance with him. The effect on Dora was dramatic. I knew she liked Laurent and that it wouldn't be long before she fell in love with him.

We watched them dance. Then towards the end of the record I danced with Mary. We put on other records and we danced without changing partners. Laurent and Dora began to talk in low voices. Dora leaned on his arm and held a thumb to her mouth as she gazed at the floor.

The record ended. I looked about me.

'Mary, why don't we go for a walk?' I asked. 'Bring your bag. I'll show you some nights spots in the area.'

'Why?' Dora breathed, still in Laurent's arms, her eyes half-closed. 'Don't go.'

But I knew she wanted us to leave; and we did, saying we would return.

We didn't; and I took Mary to no night spots. I hailed a taxi and we drove to their hotel in the Rue Cler. I said good night as she stepped down and she said good night. She banged the door and waved.

Chapter Sixteen

I HOPED Dora would cheer Laurent up for a couple of days and so cure him of his disappointment with Bibi. But there was another worry. What would happen if Dora told Laurent about last Thursday night? I decided that if she did I'd have to take my responsibilities and face whatever would follow; so I forgot about it.

On Tuesday morning, I telephoned Thérèse and asked her to tell her mother that she'd have lunch with me. Thérèse didn't sound very enthusiastic. However, she said she'd come. I told her I'd wait for her at home.

'Thérèse,' I said.

She looked up from the menu. 'Yes?'

'Give me the telephone number of your father's office.'

'What do you want it for?'

'Give me the number!'

She looked at me intently for nearly a minute with a dull, almost self-pitying expression on her face. Then she sighed.

'You want it now?'

'Yes.'

She told me the number. I repeated it, wrongly. She said it again.

'Write it in your notebook.'

'No, I'll remember it.'

She shrugged her shoulders. 'As you wish,' she said.

I made up my mind to tell her something of what I imagined she had been suspecting for some time now, that I wasn't going to marry her; that I had only amused myself with her, that I wasn't serious about marriage.

I didn't make up my mind to tell her all that, but I imagined that's what she was beginning to think. What I decided to tell her was that we couldn't get married within the time I had left. It was her father's solution. But I wasn't going to tell her that.

'Thérèse,' I said, 'I imagine you have been wondering why, up to now, the third week in July, nothing has been done about us.'

'Yes, why?'

'Many reasons. One, my papers. Two, I thought perhaps it would be unwise to take you to Africa just now. I thought I would go ahead and make preparations for your arrival. We could then get married at home. Your father said he'd like to visit Cameroon. You could come out together early in the dry season.'

'There's no question of that,' she said, suddenly recovering from the boredom she had brought with her. 'We're going together.'

'But the season, Thérèse. We'd get home when the whole place is drenched with rain, the river in flood, the forest covered with water.'

'It doesn't matter.'

She turned her eyes to the menu.

'Did I tell you that I've heard from my father?'

'No,' she said, looking up. 'What did he say?'

'He's in agreement that we should get married. Only he warned me about the rains.'

'But listen, Doumbe. What can the rains do?'

The waitress came and smiled stiffly.

'Have you chosen?' she asked.

'Green salad for me,' I said.

'And madame?'

'Me too,' Thérèse mumbled.

'And after?'

'Chicken with rice,' I said.

'And madame?'

'Two …'

'And what do you want to drink? A little wine?'

'No,' I said, and asked for a bottle of mineral water.

She wrote all what we had ordered on a block. She tore out the carbon copy and put it on our table; then she went to the kitchen.

'Were you joking?' Thérèse asked.

'About what?'

'About your having to precede me to Africa.'

'No.'

'Isn't it rather curious that it's only now you're thinking of the climate and the rains and I don't know what?'

'I've always talked to you about it, Thérèse?'

'But certainly not in the way you are talking now. Doumbe, you know what?'

'No.'

'I think you're abandoning me. Isn't it true?'

After lunch we went into the burning sunshine. Paris was gay and noisy. The café terraces were crowded. But in a week's time there'd be more than breathing space; people left Paris in August for holidays; not all; but many went away, to Spain, to Italy, to America, to Scotland, to England, to the provinces; some went to Morocco, some to Tunisia; others to Egypt. They spent their holidays in many other countries. So Paris became empty but for those French people who couldn't go away. And the tourists, from different countries. In a week's time Paris would be almost empty. The Paris of pilgrims. The Paris of monuments. A pale Paris. That was the city in which I was going to leave Thérèse. But perhaps to help her forget, her parents would take her to a dazzling holiday resort somewhere in France or abroad. They had the money. Venice. Majorca …

It was around three in the afternoon.

'What was that number again?' I asked.

'Which one?'

'Your father's. I've forgotten it. I know it's Trinité zero something—'

She reminded me of the number without a smile. In the past she would have said something. You forget everything. Or, I told you to write it down. That afternoon she simply repeated the number to me and that was that.

I said I wanted to telephone her father. As I wished, she said. I went into a café. She followed me. I told her to wait for me at the counter. She said couldn't she come with me? No, I said, and went to the basement.

I dialled the number.

'Monsieur Vaele please,' I said.

'Speaking,' Thérèse's father said, gravely.

'Bonjour Monsieur Vaele.'

'Who is speaking?'

'Doumbe.'

'Ah, how are you?'

'Very well.'

'So much the better.'

'Listen, Monsieur.'

'Yes?'

'I think I'm being invited to lunch at your place on Friday.'

'Yes indeed.'

'Good. I think I am tired of all this affair.'

'I don't understand.'

'I'll be booking my passage home tomorrow, so I want to know where I stand.'

'But nothing has changed.'

'You mean you're still against it?'

'Listen, monsieur, I explained the situation to you—'

'I know. I only wanted to know if you hadn't changed your mind.'

'Oh, no. I thought we reached an understanding?'

'We did and on Friday I'd like to discuss it. You promised you'd ask her to be patient.'

'Of course. As I said she mustn't know why you decided to do this. She's very sensitive. I don't know if you understand. *Allô!*'

'I'm listening.'

'You have to take it as a man, monsieur. After all, it is in your interest. You may not see it now, but later you'd definitely understand.'

'I don't think I agree. But it doesn't matter. On Friday.'

'Yes, on Friday ... And thanks, monsieur ...'

I went out of the telephone box. Somehow I didn't want to face Thérèse immediately.

If her father had said: Monsieur I think I have changed my mind. My daughter loves you. There's nothing I can do about it. Come home this evening. I'd like us to discuss your plans ... If her father had said that I would have hurried up the steps from the basement to take Thérèse in my arms, and even kiss her there in the café. I hadn't liked kissing before; but with Thérèse I was becoming used to it. That is what I would have done—hurried up those steps and gone and kissed her on the mouth and then whispered that I'd delay my departure for three weeks, because it would also be her departure; that we'd get married before leaving for Africa. But her father had maintained his stand. I could imagine Monsieur Vaele, emaciated, his bare forehead, his bald head. As I stood there in the basement, I could see him in my imagination. He was smoking. And perhaps during that telephone conversation he had crushed a cigarette into the ashtray. Thérèse's last hope—mine also—was that conversation with her father; the beginning of that conversation. But her father had crushed his cigarette on her last hope; not on mine, for henceforth I knew our futures were separate. My hope was Africa.

I thought of Dora and Laurent.

Meanwhile a girl had taken my place in the telephone box; and it was as if waiting for her to come out that I stood there, leaning a shoulder against the wall, thinking of Thérèse, her father, Africa, Dora and Laurent. I also thought of Mary.

I walked up to the woman who cleaned the toilettes. I gave her fifty centimes in exchange for a *jeton*. When the girl left the telephone box I went into it—to telephone Dora.

She wasn't in; but Mary was; so I asked the receptionist to let her speak.

Mary's voice was full of anxiety. She said Dora hadn't returned to the hotel. If she knew how to get to Laurent's place she would go there and find out. Did I think Dora was safe.

'Of course,' I said.

Mary thought Laurent was nervous. She was afraid. I asked her to be calm. I said I'd go and find out. I'd telephone her later in the afternoon.

When I joined Thérèse at the counter, I found her eating an ice-cream. She asked me if I didn't want something. I said no; that she should hurry up.

When we left the café I said we must go to Laurent's place.

'To do what?'

'Let's go to Laurent's place!'

She sighed, pursed her lips and gave in. Her face relaxed without losing any of its boredom, its precocious resignation.

I knocked on Laurent's door.

It was opened, by Dora.

'Oh, come in,' she said.

'Mary's worried,' I said.

'I couldn't leave Laurent,' she whispered. 'He's in a terrible state.'

'My fiancée,' I said, introducing Thérèse. 'Thérèse, an acquaintance.'

I went in, followed by Dora and Thérèse.

Laurent was lying on the bed in his leather jacket, a pair of trousers, shirt and socks. Seeing me he suddenly sprang up, wild, violent, tense.

'Get out!' his voice rang out angry and cruel, the veins in his neck showing. 'Get out!'

Dora intervened. She wrapped her arms about him and tried to pull him towards the bed. He pushed her away with one hand.

'No, Laurent,' she pleaded, returning to him. 'Laurent, don't!'

She gripped him again, and again he pushed her away, hard this time. She fell on the bed. She remained there, moaning:

'No, Laurent, don't. You'll hurt yourself. I told you to try not to get excited. Laurent—'

'I say get out,' Laurent warned me. 'If you don't get out I'll hurt you.'

'Let's go, Doumbe,' Thérèse said, taking my arm.

I turned to her and asked her to leave me alone. Then I sized up Laurent who was standing in the centre of the room, his lips distended, his face sour, his whole body tense. I smiled and made for one of the two chairs in the room. But before I knew what had happened I was in the air. Thanks to that uncle who taught me while I was a child, I mean when I was a little boy, to wrestle, I slid in Laurent's hold and passing my right foot between his legs, I wound my instep round his left leg, turned, and pulled hard. This forced his leg off the floor. My instep and ankle didn't let go even though he was pommelling my side, my left side, hard, with his fist. My instep bent his leg from the knee and since he couldn't keep me suspended in the air while standing only on one foot, he tried to throw me away. But with my instep and ankle still hooked round his leg, he couldn't throw me down without his having to fall as well.

We went down together and I sprang away from him, not wanting to hurt him; then I turned, tense and ready, waiting.

Laurent rose from the floor, wild, but cautious.

We stared at each other. I knew his fury was justified. I had no reason to fight him except in self-defence. So I waited for him to attack. But he didn't. His face clouded with despair. His jaw bones moved, his teeth showed, lips distended, as if he was going to snarl. Then he sighed. His arms fell limply on his sides. He had given up the fight or what would have been a fight for the girl he perhaps loved but whom Thérèse thought he didn't love. Bibi. Dora went to Laurent and took his arm. I relaxed.

'Laurent, come and sit down,' she said in a mildly reproachful tone. 'You shouldn't have done that.'

He followed her rather reluctantly. He sat on the bed, elbows on his knees, head in his hands. Dora sat by his side.

I looked at them for a few seconds. Then I turned to Thérèse.

'Let's go,' I said.

As we went down the stairs I told myself that it was my fault. I shouldn't have introduced Dora and Mary to Laurent, knowing one of them might talk to him about Bibi.

When we got to the pavement outside, Thérèse asked:
'What is happening?'

'He's nervous. He's jealous. It's about Bibi. I think he loves her. I think he knows that we know she doesn't want to marry him.'

'Did he think we came to make fun of him?'

'Apparently.'

'But he already has another woman.'

'She's a substitute. It doesn't change his feelings for Bibi.'

'I wouldn't have believed he loved her.'

'Now you are convinced?'

'I don't know ... And, Doumbe, who is the other girl you spoke about?'

'Mary?'

'Yes.'

'It's her friend.'

'How did you know them?'

'Like that. They were introduced to Laurent and we went to his place.'

'The four of you?'

'Yes.'

'When?'

'Last week.'

'Why didn't you tell me about it?'

'I didn't think it was important.'

'Is she pretty, the other girl?'

'No.'

'And you slept with her?'

'No.'

'Sûr?'

'Yes.'

'I don't believe you.'

'As you wish.'

After a while she said:

'I don't understand.'

'What don't you understand?'

'If you saw him last week how could he be fighting you today?'

'I'll wait for you here, Thérèse. Run and knock on his door. When they open, hold his ear and speak into it. Ask him why, if he saw me last week, he could be fighting me today? He'll tell you. Go on,' I said, pushing her gently. 'Go on, Thérèse. I'll wait for you here.'

'You're making fun of me.'

'Am I?'

'Yes.'

'Perhaps you're right.'

'You're very wicked.'

'Yes?'

'Yes.'

We walked in silence. Then I said:

'I think I've had enough of everything.'

'Of course, including me. It didn't begin today. You've always had enough of me.'

'You think so?'

'What do you want me to say?'

I put my arm on her shoulder and we went into the Underground.

As we sat on the bench, waiting for the train, Thérèse said: 'Perhaps it hurts him to see us together when Bibi doesn't want him any more ... As if it were our fault.'

'He must be very tired, and nervous.'

'What did he say last week when you went to his place?'

'He was very friendly, but perhaps it was because of the girls—'

'You call the woman I saw a girl?'

'She isn't a boy.'

'I know, but she isn't a girl either.'

'What then is she?'

'A woman.'

'Okay. He was very friendly, but perhaps it was because the women were there.'

'And what did he say about what he did at the dance?'

'He said it was a joke.'

'What a liar!'

'Now who is lying—Laurent or me?'

'Laurent of course! And you believed him?'

'Yes.'

'Of course. You say I am naïve, but I think you also are, just a bit.'

People sat on the benches on the opposite platform, men and women, a few children. Couples talked as Thérèse and I were talking, in low voices, about ourselves and others.

Doubts and oblique truths, with trust imposing modesty upon the imagination, as in Thérèse's case; for why couldn't she think of the possibility of an affair between Bibi and me? But she trusted me. She also trusted Bibi.

'What is it doing?' I asked.

'The train?'

'Yes.'

'It'll come,' she said and leaned and kissed me on the cheek.

'I always suspected he loved her,' I mused.

'Laurent?'

'Yes. I think he loves Bibi.'

'Is that why he should bear us a grudge to the point of having a fight? He isn't well. I've always said so.'

'I understand him,' I said. 'When one loves one suffers; and when one isn't strong, one breaks down, very easily. That's how it is.'

She didn't say anything. Being herself tormented with frequent attacks of depression, talk of breakdowns and suffering must have been rather frightening. And now, as if to change the subject, she asked:

'Can I know what you said to my father when you telephoned him?'

'No.'

'Why?'

'Because I don't have to report everything to you. I have the right to talk to your father, haven't I? After all, being your father, he's also mine in a way. I don't have to tell you everything as if I were a child. What do you want to know?'

'Don't be angry.'

The train pulled into the station.

Chapter Seventeen

From the Métro we went to my place. We listened to music. I didn't touch Thérèse, didn't even caress her. It was all over between us. In three days' time it would be settled over lunch.

She went home around seven o'clock.

I went to the Latin Quarter, had dinner, and then returned to Madame Bistrott's.

By ten o'clock—something rare with me—I was already in bed, fast asleep.

In the morning I began to pack.

In the afternoon I received a *pneumatique* from Thérèse. She said she was very tired and that she was feeling lonely. Why had her father been embarrassed when she asked him about the telephone call I had made to him? Was it true that I had sounded him about the possibility of our marriage taking place in Africa? She didn't know. But it seemed to her that there was something she didn't know, but which I knew, and of which I had informed her parents. Why had her mother burst out weeping when she told her what I had said at the restaurant? No! She didn't want to believe that I was letting her down. I was her life, she wound up, and she loved me.

It was Bibi who opened the door for me on Friday.

'Come in,' she said. Her voice was feeble.

We didn't shake hands. I was surprised to see how pale and bony her cheeks had become in seven days. She looked ill.

Thérèse's mother emerged from the other end of the corridor.

We met at the door of the sitting-room. We shook hands; no one smiled. Bibi left us. Thérèse's mother led me into the sitting-room and asked me to sit down. I did so and she said Thérèse was still sleeping. But she would go and wake her up. She hadn't been able to sleep during the night.

'Why? Because of the situation?'

'Yes. She's a bit shaken. I think she has begun to suspect. I stayed with her all night. She was afraid of her room. We stayed up until four in the morning. I had to persuade her to take a pill. It calmed her and made her sleep.'

'And her father?'

'He's not back yet from work.'

'What time is it?'

'It's going on for noon. He's usually not back before one.'

'If I had known I wouldn't have come so early.'

'It doesn't matter. I'll give you a drink.'

'No thanks.'

'Why?'

'Honestly no. I don't feel like it …'

'Are you sure?'

'Yes, madame.'

I rose and crossed over to the window. The Seine. I could see Sacré-Coeur in the distance.

'I'm coming,' I heard Thérèse's mother say.

I looked behind me and saw her leave the room. I turned my eyes towards the Seine. The sun; and on my right Sacré- Coeur and Montmartre.

A couple of minutes later I felt an arm on my back, then the weight of a bosom. I turned round and it was Thérèse, in a red nightdress. She was so attractive. I wanted to kiss her, on the lips; but I controlled myself. Instead I stroked her long hair which covered her shoulders and her breasts. She was slender but broad-hipped. She didn't like her hips. From the start I had been very fond of her. She had such an attractive face; simple eyes and rounded lips. But nineteen was too young, and that afternoon she looked even younger.

I continued to stroke her hair, raking my fingers through it. It was strange, that air of resigned innocence about her.

'You received my letter?' she asked me, self-pityingly.

I nodded and tried to smile.

'Wait a minute,' she said, 'I'll be back.'

I knew she had gone to change.

From my seat in the dining-room I could see the sky. It

was cloudless. Summer was over the dining table, glinting on the silver cutlery, on the bottles, on the plates.

A few moments ago, in the sitting-room, something seemed to have dissipated the impression of grim boredom of which I had been so conscious during my first visit there just over five weeks ago. Today the air was charged with a mute but festive gaiety which seemed to be waiting for us to laugh in its face, so that it could laugh back in its turn. But no one laughed. Bibi was in a navy suit. She avoided my eyes. Thérèse's mother wore a black skirt and a white poplin blouse. Her husband was in a tobacco-coloured suit. He made it his duty to look at me in the face. There was irony in his eyes. They were more ringed today than they had been during the dinner on that very table almost six weeks ago; they were also more ringed today than they had been during the dinner at the Right Bank restaurant. But he looked less tired.

Madame Vaele began to serve us in silence. Juicy and oily beetroot.

Thérèse was in a cream-coloured chiffon dress. She looked resigned.

'Monsieur,' her father said, 'July is ending—'

'Indeed,' I said.

'So where are you with your projects?' he asked.

'About Thérèse?'

'Yes. The other day we couldn't touch on the details. I mean on the telephone.'

I looked in Bibi's direction.

'I was trying—' I began to say.

'It doesn't matter,' Monsieur Vaele said. 'Bibi is one of us, she's like a sister to Thérèse. So don't mind the fact that she's here.'

Bibi smiled vaguely.

'No,' I said, 'I don't mind at all.'

'Very well,' Thérèse's father said. 'So you were saying?'

'Yes. I was saying I was trying to explain things to Thérèse—'

'Naturally,' Thérèse murmured under her breath and passed her plate to her mother who put some beetroot in it. 'Enough, *maman*.'

She put the plate down, and stared into it.

'The point is that I haven't any time left,' I went on. 'So perhaps we could arrange for Thérèse to come out say in November. You could accompany her. I don't know how you feel about it?'

'So you're bent on having the marriage take place in Africa and not here?'

'Yes, Monsieur Vaele.'

He fell silent and began to eat his beetroot.

Thérèse began to eat, listlessly.

Madame Vaele.

Bibi.

Myself. We were all eating.

From the window came the noise of traffic on the Seine. Paris droned. The sound of cars on the avenue under the window.

I looked up and wiped the oil from my lips with a napkin.

'Can't you delay your departure?' Monsieur Vaele asked, glancing at his daughter with desperate affection, his eyes full of paternal love.

'I can't see what purpose it will serve,' I said. 'In any case, I can't take Thérèse to Africa in the rainy season. Even my father wrote, warning me about the rains.'

'Yes,' Monsieur Vaele said, sombrely. 'Yes, it's the time.'

'My father was going to say I should wait until the rains were over,' I went on, 'but he changed his mind and insists that I come home at the end of the month.'

Thérèse looked up.

'Doumbe,' she said, 'you won't leave France without me. You understand? Rain or no rain we're going together. If you leave me behind I'll kill myself, you understand? Whether your parents like it or not we're going to Africa.'

'Why my parents?'

She put her elbow on the table, her head resting on her hand as she looked at me, almost contemptuously.

'Doumbe, why do you lie?' Thérèse asked. 'Tell me … Isn't it true that your parents don't want me? Isn't it true that it's they who have asked you not to bring me? Doumbe, isn't it true that it's because of your parents? They don't want us to get married? But you're twenty-three. You can do whatever you want. You're a man. If you really loved me, Doumbe, you'd ignore your parents. You can do it.'

'No, Thérèse,' I said. 'It's your parents. Not mine. Ask them.'

I sat back. Thérèse also sat back and gazed into the blood- red beetroot on her plate. Her parents had turned scarlet.

Then raising her look heavily and directing it with restrained cruelty at her father, Thérèse asked:

'Papa, is it true?'

The dining-room was clear. Monsieur Vaele's face was twisted with pain and shame and an unrelenting determination—this I imagine—not to give up the fight, a determination to win.

'Monsieur Vaele, reply to your daughter,' I told him. 'Let us get married. You won't be the first Frenchman to allow his daughter to marry an African. There are French people who have understood, after some resistance. Their daughters are in Africa. Some parents even visit them. You could do the same. You could visit us and we'd come to France from time to time. Say yes, Monsieur Vaele. I'd postpone my departure. Thèrèse and I could be married here in Paris within a fortnight. Say yes, Monsieur Vaele.'

But Thérèse's father remained silent, his chin against his Chest.

'Papa, I'm asking you,' Thérèse moaned. 'Is it true?'

'Monsieur Vaele, reply to your daughter,' I said, hoping force out of him the consent he had been withholding for Not actually to force, but to make him change his stand.

'*Maman*' the girl said, addressing herself to her mother. 'Is it true?'

Without looking at her daughter, Madame Vaele said:

'Thérèse, ask your father.'

But her father remained scarlet and silent.

Then Thérèse pushed back her chair and got up. She looked from her father to her mother, from her mother to her father. She sighed and came to me. She held out her hand.

'I understand,' she said. 'Good-bye and a safe journey … shake my hand.'

I pushed back my chair and stood up. I noticed Monsieur Vaele's face was recovering.

I took Thérèse's hand in mine.

'Thérèse shook my hand as if it wasn't I who had opened to her the joy and suffering of adult life, the dazzle and the doubts. She withdrew her hand from mine.

'*Adieu*,' she said; then, turning to her parents, she said: 'To think that you are my parents! I'm ashamed!'

'Thérèse!' her father said, looking up.

'Yes,' the girl cried. 'Yes! I'm ashamed that you are my parents!'

'I forbid you!' her father cried, springing up from his chair. 'I forbid you!'

Thérèse swung round, weeping, crying as she ran out of the dining-room:

'I'm ashamed! I am ashamed of myself!'

Madame Vaele burst out crying. Bibi maintained her calm. Monsieur Vaele looked this way and that and then glowering at me, he cried:

'*Et toi?* What are you waiting for? Get out! Go!'

My eyes briefly met Bibi's.

Chapter Eighteen

AROUND five o'clock the following afternoon, the doorbell rang. I went and opened the door. Bibi came in. I shut the door and turned the key. We went to my room.

'Sit down,' I said.

Bibi put her handbag on the table and sat down on the bed. She looked even more tired and ill than she had looked yesterday. I slumped in a chair, facing her. Thinking of the incident at Laurent's place, I smiled. I didn't want to think of Thérèse, her parents and what had happened yesterday. The memory was too painful.

'Did Thérèse tell you Laurent threw me out of his place?'

'Yes,' Bibi replied, getting up. She went to the window and looking out, she added: 'Thérèse is dead. That's what I came to tell you.' She shook her head. 'It's Madame who sent me.'

If I took the news calmly, the blow went deep. I recalled what she had said yesterday at table. Staring in front of me, I saw Thérèse in my imagination as she had been yesterday in their dining-room. Then as she had been in the sitting-room. Her red nightdress. The whole air of pity there had been about her. I had to move. I got up and went and joined Bibi at the window. I put my hands in my pockets and looked out. All I saw was sadness … Then little by little I began to see Paris again. The fragility of happiness in the prevailing despair. The cafés and the beauty and the rendezvous … Thérèse, I thought, perhaps aloud, I loved you. Yes, I did … I returned to the chair I had been occupying and sat down. Ah, Thérèse, all these oceans and deserts without horizons; these mountains that rise in dreams. Thérèse!

Bibi also turned from the window and went to the table, opened her handbag and took out a packet of cigarettes and matches. She took the ashtray from the mantelpiece and went with it to the bed. She sat down, crossed her legs and lit herself a cigarette.

She, too, felt the loss. I could see it in her eyes. Thérèse had been like a sister to her. I could see Bibi felt alone, and lost.

It was a terrible afternoon, so empty, so melancholy, as if the world had never known love, never known hope. Ah, Thérèse …

'Bibi,' I breathed, 'go and see Laurent. He may end like Thérèse. It was those sleeping pills I suppose.'

'Yes,' she said, almost in a whisper.

'I thought so.'

I could see she had been crying all day. Her eyes looked tired and they were ringed. There was a slack heaviness about her face. It seemed to me that Bibi was regretting the fact that she had betrayed Thérèse. Many people respect the dead more than the living. I thought of Thérèse's mother, and was touched by the fact that she had sent Bibi to tell me of her daughter's death. It proved how much she had come to accept our projected marriage.

'She left a message saying that you should ask your parents to forgive her,' Bibi said, gazing at the floor.

Thérèse was gone, forever. It is so hard not to be sentimental. Autumn had invaded the summer. Ah, Thérèse, all these oceans and deserts without horizons. And to have thought of my parents! Thérèse …

Bibi and I were silent for a long time. It was I who broke the silence.

'Did you talk to her about us?' I asked.

'No,' Bibi said, tapping the ashes from her cigarette into the ashtray. 'I'm happy I didn't.'

'I understand.'

'The way she told me about what happened at Laurent's place made me feel she still didn't know anything about us. What did Laurent say?'

'Nothing. He simply asked me to get out.'

'Poor boy!'

'Go and see him, Bibi. Talk to him. Tell him everything. Thérèse may not have understood why he was furious with me; but I know he knows. I introduced him to Mary and Dora. Yes I did; and I think Dora fell in love with him. She told him everything.'

'It wasn't Dora.'
'Who then?'
'I did.'
'You went there?'

She smoked for a while; then taking the cigarette between her long fingers, and blowing the smoke into the air, her head slightly thrown backwards, she said:

'Yes. On Tuesday, in the morning. I went there to tell him I couldn't marry him. I was surprised to meet Dora there. They were so embarrassed. She began to say something about my portrait which Laurent had painted. You saw it?'

'Yes.'

'Dora said what a fine portrait it was. I don't know who she was flattering, me or Laurent. I ignored her and called Laurent out and took him to a café. Then I told him.'

'That you couldn't marry him?'

'Yes.'

'What did he say?'

'He wanted to know why. I told him that it was because I was pregnant and it wasn't his child.'

'You're pregnant!'

She nodded, looking at me from the corner of her eye, and then put the cigarette into her lips. She smoked for a few seconds; taking the cigarette between her fingers, her head tilted backwards, she said: 'Yes, Doumbe, I'm pregnant and it's your child.'

The news of Thérèse's death was still on me so the fact that Bibi was pregnant, and that it was my child, seemed the most ordinary thing in the world. I showed neither surprise nor anger.

'You told him that?' I asked.

'Yes,' she said. 'He wanted to know who was the father.'

'Poor Dora,' I sighed, after a while. 'I thought it was she who had told him.'

'No. When we got to the café he was very nice. He tried to explain why Dora was there. Naturally he couldn't do so without lying since he didn't know I knew her. When she had talked about the painting she seemed to be avoiding everything that could have let him know we had met. She's a very clever woman.'

'What are you going to do?'

'Go home I guess.'

'Where? To Sweden?'

'Where else?'

I felt very tired, very weary. 'I thought you knew what you were doing, Bibi. Why did you talk of safe days?'

'The day I came here after we had nearly quarrelled in the café wasn't one of them. We shouldn't have made love.'

We fell silent. She continued to smoke. Paris droned outside. I thought for a while and decided to postpone my departure for another week, or perhaps two. I'd write to my father. Bibi wasn't alone any longer. I was in her. But with Thérèse lying dead somewhere in Paris, there were certain things I couldn't bring myself to say. Nothing to do with desire. I was thinking of Bibi's future.

She finished her cigarette and crushed the butt in the ashtray. Now she seemed to be smiling, meekly turning her eyes towards me. We stared at each other.

'Bibi.'

'Doumbe.'

'It won't be easy for me, you know?'

'I know,' she replied, good-naturedly, while still looking into my eyes from her place on the edge of the bed. 'It won't be easy for me either, especially as this will be my second child. But I'm not angry with you. Truly I'm not.'

'That's all right. We'll talk about it sometime.'

She rose and took her handbag from the table.

'Are you going?' I said.

'Yes,' she said.

I got up and went to the wardrobe. 'I'll come with you. Where's the body?'

'At the hospital.'

I took out a dark suit. I put it on the bed. A white shirt and a black tie. I put them on the bed. I undressed and changed into the white shirt and dark pair of trousers. I was between the wardrobe and the bed. Although the curtains were half drawn, no one could have seen me from the windows of the building opposite.

It was a stuffy afternoon. I put on the black tie and the

dark jacket. Then black shoes. And a handkerchief in my pocket.

'Bibi, let's go,' I said, taking my keys. 'When did she die?'

'During the night.'

About the Author

MBELLA SONNE DIPOKO was a novelist, poet, and playwright born in 1936 in Douala, Cameroon. He grew up in the Tiko region, where his father was Chief of Misaka.

He was educated at St Paul's Commercial College, Aba, where he first began writing. From 1957, Dipoko worked as a news reporter before relocating to France in 1960 and joining the editorial staff at *Présence Africaine*. His debut novel *A Few Nights and Days* (1966) earned him the reputation as a leading writer in France. He later moved to the U.S. to earn his degree in Anglo-American studies before taking up his late father's title of Chief of Misaka and returning to Tiko, Cameroon where he continued to write poetry, short stories, plays and literary criticism in French and English. He died in 2009.